# FRANKLIN E. WALES

# RESURRECTION MAN

This book is a work of fiction. Names, characters, places and incidents are either the product of the author's imagination or are used fictitiously. Any resemblance to actual events or locals or person living or dead is entirely coincidental.

Text copyright © 2019 Franklin E. Wales
Author photo copyright © 2019 Jacki Wildman Wales
Cover design copyright © 2019 Jeffrey Kosh Graphics
Author caricature copyright © 2011 D. Rano
Entire work copyright © 2019 EFW Publishing in association with Dead Light Publishing


All rights reserved. No part of this book may be reproduced or transmitted in any form or by any means, electronic or mechanical, including photocopying, recording, or by any information storage and retrieval system, without permission in writing from the copyright owner.

ISBN: 9781707400003

Dedicated to
Two lovely ladies:

My Southern Mom, Grace Wildman
and
My Southern Aunt, Dorothy Stokes


Love you both to the moon and back

*Gather round the time is near*
*There is nothing for you to fear*
*Raise your hands in prayer*
*Salvation awaits…I swear*
*RESURRECTION* from *The Book of Fallen Angels*

## 1

Let me begin by pointing out I am not the kind of guy who stands out in a crowd. When it comes to looks, I don't stand out on either the *Lookin' Good*, or *FUGLY* side. I'm honestly not much of a mixer, I don't watch much network TV or any sports, most of the music I prefer has come and gone in popularity and I don't follow politics at all. If you met me at your neighbor's Christmas party, you wouldn't recognize me at his New Year's Eve party. Unless we were introduced, that is. My parents must have known I'd turn out to be as bland as a slice of white bread—that's the only reason I can think of for giving me the name Cornelius.

If that's not enough, I'm a pathologist. I work over at the city morgue, filing away the newly arrived dead bodies. I meet new people most every day, but at least *they* have a good reason for not remembering me.

This story began on a Thursday night while I was heading home after a long day. Have you ever noticed the closer the weekend, the longer the work day seems? It was only after I left the city limits and on to the old two lane blacktop that I saw the first hand painted sign planted on the highway. Faded white with red letters proclaiming THE RESURRECTION CHURCH TENT REVIVAL, which was followed a hundred feet up the road by TWO DAYS ONLY! A smaller freshly painted sign beside it read, HARRIS FIELD 7PM! Obviously the smaller sign was repainted for every town they set up shop in. I hadn't seen that on my way to work that morning, so it must have been posted sometime today. Two days only? Nothing like a rush to redemption. Probably more like some roadside huckster lacking proper permits. They'd be in and gone before the weekly churchgoers even went to Sunday Service.

  Being raised Southern Pentecostal; I'd been to more than my share of Tent Revivals as a child. For a few years back then my Mom and Dad, rest their souls, never missed one within fifty miles. It had been better than thirty-three years since I'd attended my last. I'd been eleven, as I recall.

  From the ages of eight through eleven I was dragged to so many, I went through what I came to think of as my Tent Revival Era. You see I was eight years old when my father was diagnosed with prostate cancer. Though we had always been a weekly church going family; that was when my folks started going to every tent revival they learned about. I guess they were praying for a miracle that never came.

  I remember, near the end, asking my Dad why God didn't answer our prayers. My father was a man of great faith, even in the end days. He looked at me from his sick bed and managed a smile. "God answers every prayer," he said, his once powerful voice now small and weak. "It's just that sometimes the answer is no."

  My father passed away three weeks later. God had evidently said, *no*. Mom kept taking me to church for two more years, although the tent revivals were never on her agenda again.

At thirteen I convinced her I was big enough to stay home alone. Truth was I was still pissed at God for taking my Dad from me.

Mom took two jobs to make ends meet. It was her dream for me to attend Med School. She passed on a couple years back, but she saw me complete her dream of school. The doctors said she had a damaged heart. *No Shit.* I think it was exhaustion and heartache that killed her. About six months before she died I was visiting her at the facility she lived in when round the clock care became needed. She knew even then she was near her own end of her days. "Corney," she said, recalling her childhood name for me. "I know you still hold a grudge, but give God a chance again, someday."

I nodded.

"Promise me."

I promised.

When the turn for the old Harris Farm came up, I took it. It wouldn't hurt to see what all the fuss was about. The Harris Farm had been razed a decade earlier after it had been abandoned for nearly as long. The property now was no more than a large empty field. Too far from town to develop, and too near to town to farm. As I drove in, I wondered how much had changed since I was a kid. How much razzle-dazzle had been added with all the new technology since then.

Turns out I needn't have wondered. It wasn't much to look at. In fact, I'd seen flashier run outfits as a child. A well-worn and well patched canopy tent with maybe thirty folding chairs set up underneath it had been erected. A white and rust box truck (that most likely began its life as a rental truck twenty or so years earlier) was parked across the rear of the tent. A banner with the words RESURRECTION SPOKEN HERE, hand painted in faded red hung on the side of the truck, making an interesting, if low budget backdrop. In front of this, two sheets of plywood had been placed atop several cement blocks making a makeshift stage. A sheet music stand with a well-worn black covered book on it stood in place of a pulpit.

Behind the truck, out from under the tent, an old generator sat waiting to give electric life to a series of extension cords and bare light bulbs that would light the tent after dark. Leaning against the rear tires, taking advantage of the shade cast by the canopy in the late afternoon sun a haggard old man wearing a filthy old wife beater tank top napped. Even in sleep he looked more like a well-seasoned Carney than a man of the cloth.

Whoever he was, he was a light sleeper. As I crept my car slowly closer, he sat bolt upright.

"Help you?" he asked.

"You the pastor?"

He laughed. "No sir, not at all. The Prophet is tending to some business in town. He'll be here tonight though. Seven o'clock."

"Prophet?"

"It's what he goes by. You coming?"

"I might," I said.

"Good. Good. See you tonight." With that he tipped his head down and closed his eyes.

Even from that distance I could smell the whiskey seeping out through his pores. I drove off. I still consider myself a spiritual man, even though I do not attend any church. My upbringing never left me, I guess. I just don't have much use for organized religion, so I avoid churches in general. Especially those "Super Churches." They seem to be all about their flashy suits and new cars. For me they are more *in* the God Business, than *doing* God's business.

The fleabag operation known as The Resurrection Church Tent Revival, might not appeal to the upper-crust, but it got my attention. After all, John the Baptist didn't have a pot to piss in during his lifetime. The deep down truth was, The Resurrection Church Tent Revival looked a lot like those we had attended as a family so many years before. I knew before I had hit the main highway I'd be back. I would finally fulfill my promise to my mother.

When I returned at around a quarter to seven there were probably a dozen people seated in the folding chairs. I was pretty sure that would be about the best this show would get with no advance publicity. If the self proclaimed Prophet was any good, he'd do better tomorrow from word of mouth. There was no doubt in my mind that no permit had been pulled. Why else dash in and out in two days?

The generator had been moved about a hundred feet away and covered with a wooden frame to muffle its sound. The old timer I'd seen earlier was seated facing the audience near a CD player piping out classical music instead of gospel. Even dressed in a well-worn suit and tie, he looked as if he'd be more comfortable shouting "win the little lady a teddy bear!" down some carnival midway.

The "Prophet" appeared at seven o'clock sharp from behind a side curtain to the left of the stage. Sporting long dark hair and a beard, dressed in a tattered tan robe and sandals, he looked for all the world like a thrift-store version of Jesus-H-Hanging-On-The-Cross-Christ. I knew then it was more hustle than gospel that would be going on, but good manners prohibited me from leaving that very moment. On a second glance I realized the *Prophet* was a good deal older than Christ had been. Jesus died at 33. That's why the paintings of him have him looking so smooth skinned. The bags under this guy's eyes had bags. He looked every bit to be in the mid-fifties of a life spent working in the heat of the sun. Still, the attire helped the illusion along nicely.

The whole thing took an hour and a half. It wasn't the worst I'd experienced, but it was damn close. It was however, undoubtedly the strangest. The Prophet (who never gave his name) worked his tiny stage like the best Pentecostal I'd ever seen. His voice rose and lowered at the right times, punctuating several lines in a loud bellow. Growing up in America's Bible-Belt I had expected a healthy dose of references to *Jeez-us*, but got none. Instead he said "My Lord" (pronounced *My Lawd*, in true Southern Pentecostal fashion) *My Lawd will set you free: My Lawd will grant you eternal life over death, My Lawd knows the desires of your heart*, and so on, as if he had the exclusive on the Lord (or Lawd, as it were).

There were no crosses anywhere, none of the religious flash one came to expect. The man never even opened the large black book on his music stand pulpit. Some preachers dilute the Gospel so that one would think he was drinking low fat and not whole milk. This was NO fat milk. Religious maybe, but Christian? Not quite. And sure as hell he was no damn Prophet.

Even the music that played on the CD player during the service was void of spirit. It was canned generic organ music, the kind that's supposed to sound like something you'd hear in a large cathedral, but not quite. It was absolutely hollow when it came to spirit. From what I saw, heard and felt, the Holy Spirit hadn't even made the trip in.

In spite of the watered down lifeless show there was one tall blonde woman, the kind Ray Stevens once called Sister Bertha Better-Than-You (dressed in a fire engine red dress and a big floppy hat to match) who stood, raised her hands to the air, and sank (ever-so cautiously I might add) to the ground. I know the kind from my formative tent revival years; Sister Bertha was the type who went to church so *you* could see how tight *she* was with God. Fortunately Mr. Carney-in-a-suit was right there with a damp cloth to rub her face and arms with before leading her back behind the curtain the Prophet had made his entrance from. As she passed, the Prophet reached out and held her hand for a split second, as if consoling her.

Maybe I had been out of the church loop for too long, but the neckline on Sister Bertha's red dress seemed to plunge a little low, and the material seemed a little too clingy for a church service. To me, at least, it seemed the kind of dress worn to attract all eyes on the wearer. For someone recently "slain in the spirit" she walked with a little too much backfield in motion as she was lead backstage. Before she disappeared completely behind the curtain, the Prophet walked to her as he preached and held her hand again. She went from looking exhausted, to looking a bit surprised. Maybe she didn't expect him to bring even more attention to her. Not that I believe she minded.

When he returned, Mr. Carney-in-a-suit had an old basket he passed around for donations. That was it. No alter call, no witness for the *Lawd*, nothing. I dropped five bucks in the basket and walked out to my car as the Prophet was promising a night of miracles the following evening. "If you need a blessing, if your family needs a blessing, if your neighbor needs a blessing, if someone at work needs a blessing," he near shouted, "then bring them here tomorrow night and witness the wondrous blessings my *Lawd* shall bestow!"

"And if any dead presidents in your wallets and purses need a blessing, bring them along," I mumbled as I started my car.

"Sorry, Mom," I told the empty air. "I gave it a shot." I didn't live that far away. There was still time to get home, pour myself a double bourbon and enjoy a chapter or two of *The Big Sleep* by Raymond Chandler. It was the first book to feature Philip Marlowe and I'd read it countless times before. That was my one vice, my one weakness. Not only the works of Chandler, but Mickey Spillane, John D. MacDonald and Lawrence Block, among others. Recently I added a guy named Paul D. Marks to my reading list. I just never got tired of hardboiled detective type stories. I read them over and over. Somehow those books always went better with a double bourbon. It kinda set the mood.

That wasn't always my life. I had married young to my childhood sweetheart, Mary. Full of wonder and belief in the future, we forged our plan. I was going to medical school. Eventually we decided on my career as a Medical Examiner. Honestly, because it didn't require as much money or schooling to learn to work on the dead as it did the living.

Mary worked two jobs to help keep us above water; that is until she became pregnant with our daughter, Caroline. The first couple of years were wonderful. Then, around Caroline's third birthday stress cracks began to appear in our marriage. As I mentioned, we married young. Too young. As we began to mature into our own, we grew apart. Shortly after Caroline's fifth birthday, we divorced.

We stayed friends, remarkably. For five years we shared custody. I figured Caroline had it better than the children of most divorced parents. Mary began dating a lawyer a couple years after we split. Mark was his name. Nice guy. A real up and comer in the field of defense law. Got offered a prime position in a Boston firm. When Mary asked if I would be willing to have Caroline on summer vacation only, I agreed.

When we divorced, I got myself a small one bedroom apartment, which I still live in. Never seemed to be any reason to move on. My job was good, my daughter was nearby. Even when Mary moved them to Boston, I saw no reason to move. The apartment was home. I dated some, but nothing permanent. Just never saw the need to share life with anyone else again. I guess I'm kind of a homebody. Probably why I work with dead people. I have my time to myself, and my books to keep me company. It suits me fine.

Caroline turned out wonderful. Thanks to Mark she received the best education Boston had to offer and was now studying law at Harvard. We talk on weekends. Mary and I still call each other on our birthdays and at Christmas. Like I said, my life is simple and reclusive, but it suits me.

## 2

I woke the next morning, none the worse for wear and went to work; The Resurrection Church Tent Revival the furthest thing from my mind.

When my cell phone went off about an hour after I had arrived at work, and I saw it was Doc Harvey calling, a pit formed in my stomach. "Hey Harvey," I said with false cheer. "What's up?"

"Your test results came in," he said without emotion. "You need to come by my office so we can go over them."

I looked around the room. It was a slow day. I couldn't even use work as an excuse. Harvey was my doctor and he kept an office on the hospital grounds. "I'll be right over."

Since my father had died from Prostate cancer, I got tested every year right after my birthday. Every year Harvey called to tell me everything looked good. The fact that he wanted to talk was not a good sign.

The long and the short of it was that there would be more tests to be sure. (Wasn't there always?) Harvey finished by telling me that he couldn't tell me how long I had *if* I followed the program, but if I chose to do nothing, "I'd give you six months, tops," he said, "if the original tests prove accurate."

"You don't trust the original tests?" I asked.

"Let me make a few calls. How about we talk about this again on Monday," he said. "It wouldn't be a bad thing to run some more tests."

I shook my head. "You have a good weekend, too," I said.

"Cornelius," he said. Harvey was one of the few people to actually use my full name when addressing me.

Realizing I was wrong, I shook my head. "No Harvey, I'm sorry that was not called for it's just that…" the words left me. All rational thought left me. I felt empty.

"I know," he said. "It's not a problem."

I called my assistant Roger from the parking lot and told him I was taking the rest of the day off. I drove down to the park, fed a few birds. Thought about the empty life I had led and wondered why I cared that I wouldn't leave a mark after I was gone. Truth was, I decided, I'd been too busy with the day to day mundane to look beyond it. I thought about going home, but to what? To the same little apartment I'd known for decades? To Raymond Chandler and bourbon whiskey? I realized that until I knew with absolute certainty, I had absolutely no one I would share my possible bad news with. No one at home to worry with until the next tests. No one to care.

Eventually I pulled out my cell phone and called Mary. She was pretty confused why I'd call when it wasn't Christmas or her birthday. I apologized for the unscheduled call and told her I'd had a bad day and was feeling blue. She told me to hang in there. What did I expect? You just don't call your ex of twenty years and tell her you probably have cancer. You just don't dump that crap on someone who hasn't shared your life for two decades because you're looking for sympathy. That's just selfish. She had moved on in her life, and I could have. I chose not to and now I was alone, looking at the end of the road and wishing I'd done otherwise. I found myself wishing I'd done a lot of things different, now that my story was going to end. But fact was, I hadn't.

I scrolled through the contacts in my phone until I came to Caroline's number. I stared at it a long time before I closed it out. There were still questions, tests to be run; Harvey had said so himself. Of course he told me honestly he was certain in his opinion. But he had told me that, if he was right, I had six months if I did nothing. I wasn't dead yet. Looking at the finish line, perhaps, but not crossing it for a while yet.

No, you didn't call your ex and you damn sure didn't call your daughter because a doctor had told you he *thought* you had cancer. No, you sucked it up. You made a plan, and if the tests showed this to be true, *then* you told people. Then and only then did you begin to wrap your life up in a tight little package and make sure there were no loose ends.

I thought about my heroes: Chandler, Spillane, Block, MacDonald and Marks. Well not about them per se, but about the men they wrote about, the fictional characters I had shared so many hours and adventures with. What would Philip Marlowe, Mike Hammer, Matthew Scudder, Travis McGee, Duke Rogers and a lifetime of others do?

I drove down to the package store and bought myself a fifth of Jesse James American Outlaw Bourbon and a pack of Marlboro cigarettes. The first cigarette went down hard. I hadn't smoked in nearly fifteen years, but the danger seemed minimal now. The second was a reunion with an old friend. I placed the bourbon on the seat unopened, fired up my third smoke, and went driving.

I hadn't planned to revisit The Resurrection Church Tent Revival, It certainly wasn't my idea of a good Friday night, but when I reached the Harris Field cutoff at five to seven I just pulled in. I don't know that I was expecting a blessing or a miracle, even though the Prophet promised both the previous night. After all, it hadn't helped my father. But maybe deep down inside, I was hoping it would for me; hedging my bet, so to speak.

Evidently I was the only one unmoved from the previous night's sermon. When I got closer I realized the field was full of parked cars. I saw most of the faces I remembered from the night before. Sister-Bertha-Better-Than-You was in attendance again, and still wearing that same red dress and floppy hat. She had taken a seat in the second row, center stage, while I took mine several rows behind her, nearer the back. I halfway wondered if she was a plant for the Prophet.

The service was the same politically correct generic service as it was the previous night and I didn't find it any more inspiring the second time around. Instead I found myself trying to build a story around Sister Bertha. I pegged her to be in her mid-thirties. The shining glint of a gold band on her left ring finger told me she was married—but where was her husband?

Sometimes at work I look at the body on my table and try to imagine a life story that fits the recently deceased. It's not something you talk about at parties, but I've learned that I'm not the only one in my field that does it. It's kind of a stress reliever when you deal with death day in and day out. A way of humanizing the corpse before you, so that they don't become just another job to do.

Only Sister Bertha wasn't dead, so I let my imagination run its own path without any second thought. She had two children in their early teens. A boy and a girl, of course. They were too old to force into coming to a religious service, so they were up to their own diversions at home. Most likely eyes glued to their Smart Phones. The husband was obviously a drunk. That's what brought her here. The Prophet had promised a night of blessings and miracles and Sister Bertha came for the miracle that her drunkard husband would see the light and throw away the bottle. That of course and to show people just how tight she really was with God. So tight, in fact, that the Almighty would place the tip of His finger upon her, and she once again would be slain in the spirit.

As if on cue, Sister Bertha stood, raising her arms palms up over her head and stepped into the aisle. Seeing this Mr. Carney in a Suit got quickly to his feet and moved around behind her. Realizing his purpose, Sister Bertha dropped like a sack of potatoes, trusting she would be caught. She was; and was then eased to the floor before being 'revived' with a damp cloth from Mr. Carney's pocket. Once again he led her back stage before coming back and passing the basket. I dropped another fiver and quietly got up.

I stood, just outside the tent and watched as the Prophet wound up and called everyone seeking a blessing to come forward. Sister Bertha, now composed, came around the tent flap and was first in line. I used all the commotion to head to my car. I wasn't about to beg for a cure for cancer. It sure hadn't helped my Dad, and I had serious doubts the Prophet had even a passing acquaintance with God Almighty.

Instead, I went home, cracked open my Bourbon, lit a fresh cigarette and proceeded to drink myself into a stupor. Looking at the final Exit Stage Left, there were a lot of things I needed to take care of, but it wasn't the night. I had at least six months for that.

I awoke Saturday with a bear of a hangover. It had been a good ten years since I'd earned my last one of those. A mini James Brown was holding a concert in my brain, my lungs hurt like hell, my stomach was threatening to vacate anything I even thought to put in it and of course someone had snuck in while I was asleep and took a dump in my mouth. A quick steaming shower followed by a cold rinse cleared my head. I would live to fight another day.

I drove to Mickey-D's for a coffee and a McMuffin, which my stomach surprisingly did not object to. I called Harvey at home and arranged an early pre-work meeting Monday to discuss my next steps. While I was on the phone, I found the old habit had returned as if it had never left and I wanted a cigarette, but decided smoking while talking to Harvey about cancer was not a good idea. My time, what I had left, and what to do with it were front and center. The Resurrection Church Tent Revival was the furthest thing from my mind.

It might have ended there, if "Sister Bertha" hadn't shown up on my table a couple days later.

## 3

I had just come back from my chat with Harvey as he explained my options for treatment ahead should the follow-up tests prove his diagnosis true and found a new customer waiting on my examining table. She'd been dropped off while I was discussing the possibility of prostrate surgery. My assistant Roger had signed her in, prepped the body for examination, and gone to lunch. Not that I blamed him. Part of our job was determining time and cause of death. Time I'd have to work on, but cause was easy. Her throat had been slit in the proverbial ear to ear sense. I took a look at her ankles and sure enough there were rope burns. Given the amount of blood under her ears and in her matted blonde hair, combined with the rope burns, it was pretty obvious she'd been hung upside down and bled out.

It was shaping up to be a bad Monday.

My first thought was that we had a psycho in our midst. My second is her face seemed somehow familiar. According to the paperwork she was one Pat Samson of 432 Randle Court, age thirty-seven. I looked in the box of her belongings to find a fire engine red dress and floppy hat. *Sister Bertha*. My third thought was the shame one felt from making fun of the recently deceased.

According to the notes, even though she was a local woman her body had been dropped off by County. I grabbed the phone on the desk and dialed called Detective Jackson. It was her area and if she didn't send the body in, she'd know who did.

"Jackson," she said after the second ring.

"Hi Betty, it's Cornelius," I said, then added out of habit, "Medical examiner over at City Hospital."

There was a chuckle on the other end of the line. "You know, Doc," she said, "unless you change your job, all you gotta do is give me your name. How many guys named Cornelius do you think I know?" She chuckled again. "What can I do for ya, Doc?"

"I've got Pat Samson on my table. Notes says County brought her in."

"The blond woman with her throat slashed?" She asked. "Whatcha need to know?"

"She was a local woman. How did you guys come to bring her in?"

There was a pause and the sound of papers shuffling. "Body was found by a hiker on a day trip about ten miles out of town. She had been buried in a very shallow grave with her hat and purse beside her. Seems the guy saw a bit of that red dress she was wearing poking up through the dirt and since her purse was with her, we knew she was one of your citizens."

I thought carefully about what I wanted to say. When I didn't respond fast enough, Betty asked, "Why? You know her, Doc?"

"No, I don't know her, but I did see her a couple nights ago at a tent revival out in Harris Field."

More paper shuffling. "That squares with what we know," she said. "Husband reported her missing Saturday. Said she went to that revival and had called him, saying she was going out for coffee with some others after the service."

"And?"

"That's it. So far we haven't found anyone else who attended. How many were there, Doc?"

"Maybe thirty or forty, as I remember. I didn't actually talk to anybody."

"Never pictured you as a religious man, Doc."

Shame washed over me. "I'm not, really. Stopped in mostly out of curiosity."

"So how come you recognized her, if you didn't know her?"

It was my turn to chuckle. "You mean besides that flaming red dress and floppy hat? She was one of those Holy Rollers. You know the kind, draw attention to themselves by falling out during the service, like God touched 'em personally."

"That's what her husband said, too. I guess I don't need to ask you about cause of death."

"Throat slit," I said. "First guess due to the blood matting her hair was she was hung upside down and bled out. I checked her ankles. They show signs of rope burn."

"One sick bastard, eh Doc?"

"That's my first call."

"Have you determined time and day of death?"

"Not yet. I just took a quick look. I'll get back to you on time. Based on the first glance, I wouldn't rule out it happening the same night as the revival."

"Well if it was a psycho traveling preacher, at least it ain't local. I'm gonna ask around within a hundred mile radius, see if anyone else has found anything similar, though you'd think it would have made the news. Pretty damn sure this one will." She paused. "Did you get the name of the preacher?"

"No," I admitted. "I don't remember him giving it, but there was a sign that said The Resurrection Church Tent Revival. They had an old white box truck, maybe a formal rental. I remember because it looked like a pretty fleabag operation. He looked like a low budget Jesus, though. Right down to the worn out white robe and sandals." I paused for a moment, grabbing a memory of that Carney guy before the evenings show. "I think I heard somebody call him 'The Prophet."

"Great," she said. "Look, Doc, I gotta get, but I was wondering, you still a Bourbon drinker?"

I said I was.

"I was thinking we should get together for a drink sometime."

"That sounds like a plan," I said. "Just let me know when."

"Okay," she said. "Let me know the official word when you got it, okay?"

I assured her I would and rang off.

I'd known Betty Jackson professionally for eight years and as a personal friend for seven of them. Five years back we decided to take it to the next level and began dating. Like all new relationships it burned white hot in the beginning. A couple months in, it became obvious that it wasn't going to work out. It wasn't like we didn't get along, truth was we got along fine. It was just that we both realized we'd lived alone too long and had become set in our ways. Sharing our lives 24/7 with another human being was not something either of us really wanted. We decided it was best to let it go rather than to try and force it.

When April rolled around that next year, Betty called me up. It was my birthday and she wanted to take me out for a steak dinner. The next morning, when we awoke at her place I asked her if she thought it was a good idea to sleep together again, since we knew it wasn't going any further.

"I've been thinking about it," she said. "We're good friends and we're good lovers. We are just a lousy couple."

I was puzzled. "And?"

"And I figured that there is no reason we need to give up the good parts and try to force the lousy part to work. Why can't we agree to see each other on our birthdays, if it works out, and maybe New Year's Eve?"

Betty's parents are still alive and each Thanksgiving and Christmas she flies out to spend time with them. "Being alone on New Year's Eve is a bummer," she explained. "I'd much rather spend it with someone I care about, even if I know I can't spend the rest of my life day in and day out with that person."

It sounds weird, I know, but it worked for us. After a couple years our birthday dinners became birthday weekends spent holed up in a hotel on a beach somewhere. That wasn't our only time together. Now and again one of us would call the other and suggest a drink, like she just had. A drink actually meant a night alone together, usually at her place. So we actually got together maybe five or six times a year. We often joked that when we retired neither of us would be able to afford to live on our retirement and we'd probably *have* to move in together then. Of course with prostate cancer now in my future, I knew that would probably never happen. Once I'd told Mary and Caroline, I knew I'd have to share it with Betty as well.

It wasn't always about sex. Sometimes we just called because we needed a friend. When Betty's brother died, we talked until nearly one in the morning. Just friends. It's odd, I know, but it worked for us. We were both already married to our jobs and our relationship was more like a side affair.

After I hung up, I returned to the examining room to find Sister Bertha's eyes open and staring at me. Startled, I blinked and looked again. Her eyes were closed, but for a moment there, I did believe they had been looking at me. Not the sunken, flat, dead eyes of a corpse, but the bright living orbs of a live person. *Pat Samson*, I reminded myself. Her name was Pat Samson.

I went through the motions and required investigations, but I had already determined cause of death, and that red dress and hat left me no doubt it had been two nights previous. There were still lots of things that needed to be checked: The way the blood settles by gravity in the body, a purple discoloration that happens, the corneas get cloudy. You can even look at the stomach for the food left behind. But the purple rope burns around the ankles and the red hat and dress were enough for me.

I had just finished my report when Roger came back from lunch. "I'm going home," I said. "It's been a long day, already."

Halfway home I realized I was not alone in my car. When I looked to my right, the passenger seat was empty, of course, but when I used my peripheral vision, I saw her there; red hat, dress, and all. I even saw when she covered that second smile slashed across her throat with her hand.

"I don't mind," she said, her voice low and guttural. I figured it was from air seeping in through the throat gash.

I figured out pretty quickly that this was my subconscious mind trying to forgive myself for making fun of her in my mind at the revival. That being the case, I decided to play along with it. "What?" I asked my empty car.

"That you think of me as Sister Bertha."

The voice seemed so real, I looked again at the passenger seat. It was still empty. "You were right about me," she said when my eyes had returned to the road. "I was always looking for attention my whole life. Maybe it was because I was a middle child, I don't know. I did things to make people notice me, to *see* me. Now look at me." She laughed sadly and went quiet for a moment.

"You were right about my kids, too. One boy and one girl and they practically live on their cell phones."

There was the tiniest gurgling sound and from the corner of my eye I saw that a little blood had seeped from under her hand and down her neck.

"You were all wrong about my husband, though," she continued. "Jeff's not a drunk. He rarely even takes a drink. I think my actions keep, *kept* him away. He is not the type of man who wants to be the center of attention, but he knew I needed it."

"Sorry," I said.

"Oh, it's okay. I just wanted you to know the truth about my husband."

"Who did this to you?" I asked. *Hey if you're going to play head games by yourself, you might as well go all in.*

She scoffed. "That Prophet, of course. That godless, soulless Prophet. But you knew that." She paused again, letting that sink in. "That's the real reason I'm here."

"Beg pardon?"

"Only you saw that bastard. Only you can stop him from doing it again."

"I'll think about it," I said.

And then as quick as she'd arrived, she was gone.

*Great*, I thought. I trade guilt over thinking mean things to some twisted responsibility to find the guilty party and hold them accountable. I wasn't a cop. I didn't solve mysteries. That was Betty and her brethren's job.

I turned up the radio to an ear splitting level and pushed all thoughts from my mind the rest of the way home. When I finally got there, Jesse James and I went a few rounds. He won as I knew he would, and I went to bed without even bothering to shower.

The rest of the week were uneventful, which, given the Monday I'd had, wasn't a bad thing. Harvey didn't call and Sister Bertha didn't return. Even so, I was as tight as a banjo string, waiting for either. Finally Friday arrived and I was looking forward to another boring weekend of laundry, food shopping and movies at home. Betty had hinted about getting together soon, but I wasn't ready for that, yet. Maybe after I had my head around the cancer thing, but definitely not before.

I picked up another bottle of the Outlaw's Bourbon and a McDonalds #5 before heading home. TBS was running a special Raymond Chandler night featuring *Lady in the Lake*, *Murder, My Sweet* and of course the best Chandler adaptation ever, *The Big Sleep*, starring Bogart and Bacall. I settled in for a night of entertainment and wound up passing out drunk before *The Big Sleep* was halfway through.

## 4

I awoke with the second Saturday hangover in as many weeks, stripped off my clothing from the day before and headed straight to the shower.

After fifteen glorious minutes of near scalding water, I was awake, my head was clear and my sinuses open.

One of the perks of living alone is you don't have to wear your towel outside of the bathroom. After I'd dried, shaved, combed my hair and brushed the last of previous evening's bourbon out of my mouth, I hung up the towel and stepped into the hall heading for my bedroom closet. After I had selected a comfortable pair of jeans and a dark blue polo shirt, I turned around and dropped my clean clothes on the floor.

Sister Bertha was sitting on my bed! Beside her sat another woman, a black woman in a cream colored pantsuit with a powder blue blouse underneath. She looked to be in her early forties and would have been considered pretty, if not for that side to side gash across her throat.

Suddenly aware of my nakedness, I dropped my hands to cover myself. "W-who are you?" I asked.

The black woman looked as if she was trying to talk but no sound came out. Sister Bertha nudged her and covered her own throat with her hand. "Like this," she croaked in that bubbling broken voice. It sounded a little like those people do with that electronic voice box used after throat cancer.

She covered her wound. "Susan Applewhite," she said.

I knew I was not really seeing or hearing this. I knew it must still be a bourbon dream and I was still fully dressed, asleep in my bed.

As if reading my mind, which I guess she was, Sister Bertha shook her head. "No Doc," she said, "you are not dreaming, and you're not crazy."

"But why me?"

"Because you are the only one who can see us. You see me because we made a connection, somehow. You see her because that dammed Prophet did her like he did me." She patted Susan on the hand. "She hasn't quite accepted it, but it's early."

"But I don't remember her."

"Of course not. He did her last night. A little town called Milford: a few hundred miles southwest of here. I found her wandering in the abyss I've been in. I brought her to you."

"There's two of you?"

"Doc there's a whole lot more than just two of us. The others came before me, and I can't bring them to you."

"Why do you want to?"

"Because you can stop him. Because you know about him, about what he is. I've told you how he murdered me. He murdered Susan the same way."

"Why *me*?"

"Because you can see me. See us."

"And nobody else can? What about your husband? What about her husband?"

"She's not married. Lived alone, no one to even miss her this soon." Sister Bertha shook her head sadly. "Do I really have to spell it out for you, Doc? I'm dead. Susan is dead."

"What's that got to do with me?"

"Cancer, Doc. You've got cancer. One foot in this world, one foot in ours."

The world started to blur around me. I hadn't even begun my second round of tests and yet Sister Bertha was telling me I was *half dead already*. Was I really going to take this as fact from a ghost, when even my own flesh and blood doctor hadn't signed off? I blinked my eyes, trying in vain to clear the world around me. I forgot my modesty and put a hand on my dresser to steady myself. It didn't work. I sunk to the floor and blessedly passed out.

I woke two hours later in an empty bedroom.

Fever. That had to be it. I looked around the room, there was nobody there. No Sister Bertha, no Susan Applewhite. Fever. That was the ticket.

I got up, not bothering to dress and went to the kitchen for coffee. I punched up my laptop while the Keurig went to work.

Sipping my first cup of coffee, I spied the half smoked pack of cigarettes left over from the drunken night still on the table. I lit one and relished how good it went with the coffee. Over my second smoke I hit Google and searched for *The Resurrection Church Tent Revival*. I found a number of churches listed as the Resurrection Church and a tent load of revivals, but none fit the description of what I was after. I moved on to Bing, Yahoo, even Firefox. Still nothing. Not even a Facebook page. What kind of church didn't at least have a Facebook page?

*The kind that didn't want to be known*, a small voice inside me answered.

When The Resurrection Church Tent Revival didn't show up, I began reading blog posts about generic tent revivals. I found one posting on an open community page dedicated to tent revivals that was exactly what I was looking for:

*Last night our little town received the "blessing" of hosting The Resurrection Church Tent Revival just outside the Bridgeport, West Virginia city limits*, the author wrote. *It had to be the most rundown, saddest excuse for a worship of the Lord I have ever seen. A tattered tent with folding chairs. A beat up old moving truck that served as a backdrop, even a preacher (who never gave his name) that dressed like a cheap assed version of Jesus. The service was lackluster. The man never mentioned Jesus by name, not even once. The music was classical CDs, not hymns. But they made sure to pass the plate. The preacher promised blessings and miracles to anyone who returned for their second performance tonight. I'm not going.*

That was it, I was sure of it. Problem was it was posted three years back. Two years ago another user had commented: *This little tin cup traveling show came through our town the last two nights. I agree wholeheartedly with your review. AVOID AT ALL COST!* So this little ramshackle road show had been at it for some time.

I couldn't find any way to contact either of the posters. It was a long shot, but I posted a note asking anyone who had seen The Resurrection Church Tent Revival to please contact me and listed my email.

Neither of the postings had mentioned anything about murder or missing persons. Why should they? It was just a couple of low rent hustlers scamming God's people out of their hard earned dollars. From the age of the posts, it looked like they'd been in business a few years, at the very least. Going against my better judgment, I searched out the town of Milford, as Sister Bertha had mentioned. Turned out it *was* several hundred miles southwest of me. That didn't really mean anything. It certainly didn't mean the ghost of Sister Bertha told me that fact. I probably knew it already from somewhere else, and my brain just threw it out there. Even so, I did a search of their police blotter and local news. Of course an adult vanishing the night before wasn't likely to make the news right away. A child, sure, but not an adult.

I did a web search for the name Susan Applewhite and came up with a Facebook page and nothing else. The photo was a cartoon of Minnie Mouse, and her page hadn't been posted on for nearly a month, but then again, neither had my own. We did however share a half dozen mutual friends. Nobody I really knew, just mutual friends from the *Hit It Rich* casino games. I was ready to quit the whole thing until I noticed one more item on Susan Applewhite's page: *She lived in Milford.*

I shut the laptop down. If I had to have some weird psychic vibe, why couldn't it be the lottery numbers? I still wasn't buying this visit from beyond because I had one foot already over there business. It had to be stress over the cancer scare.

*Then how did you know the name Susan Applewhite? And how did you know she was from Milford?*

I lit another cigarette and looked across the kitchen counter to the bottle of bourbon there. I didn't like the questions the voice in my head asked. If I didn't have the answers, perhaps Jesse James did. Bourbon and coffee always went well together. I was pretty sure bourbon and coffee for breakfast would lead to bourbon and cola for lunch, followed up by bourbon straight for dinner. If the cancer didn't kill me, I might just die from liver failure.

Besides, there wasn't enough in the bottle to last all day. I'd have to go to the store before I started in with another showdown with Jesse James again.

I picked up my cell and called Harvey. He informed me that it would be a week or so before he could schedule the next round of tests, but he'd let me know as soon as he had them booked.

The bottle called to me from across the room.

I got dressed and headed out. I really didn't have anywhere to be, but I was pretty sure before it was over I'd stop at a liquor store before I got back home.

I drove around aimlessly for a few hours before stopping at Margie's, a little homegrown diner my daughter Caroline and I used to frequent when she spent my part of her summer vacation Saturdays with me. Caroline loved the banana splits they made there. I ordered one after consuming one of Margie's locally famous cheeseburgers.

Being at the little diner brought back a ton of warm memories. When I left there I went to the park, where Caroline and I had spent so many wonderful summer afternoons. I found the picnic table we often sat at under the shade of a mighty tree, and took a seat. For the first time in years, I actually sat still and enjoyed the beautiful day. I wondered how I'd let so many days pass away into years all caught up in the day to day grind as to miss this, damn near in my own backyard.

I thought of Caroline and the games we played together here. Early on, I had been the knight in shining armor and she the princess in distress. Later it was kites and catch. Always it was with a thermos of lemonade and a bag of pretzels. (She had always been partial to the miniature knots.) We never packed a picnic lunch as we went to Margie's Diner first. Rather than feel sadness, I found myself wrapped up in wonderful nostalgic memories. I truly felt *alive* for the first time since those magical days of my daughter's childhood. For a while (while it was still fun to be with Dad) we even played chess. Caroline was a master strategist early on. It's why I've always believed she would be a topnotch lawyer one day.

I actually felt I had purged myself of the dead women guilt hallucinations I'd been having. My heart was full of good memories, and my mind at ease. I took out my cellphone and called Mary. We were a long time divorced, but she would always be my oldest, truest friend. She answered on the third ring.

"Corney," she said. "Is everything all right?"

I could tell you that we'd always had that kind of bond. The kind when we knew what each other was thinking, but the truth was I hardly ever called. "Hey Mary, got a minute?"

I told her about Harvey's concern. I told her of the following tests still being waited on. She listened. Mary was good at that. She didn't mention the elephant in the room, being it was what killed my father. She asked me if I was scared.

"I don't know," I admitted. "I think so, sometimes. Not right now, though. That's why I called. I would have never called you to cry on your shoulder."

"You can, you know," she said. "Anytime."

"I know and I thank you for that."

"When are you going to tell Caroline?"

"When I get the results on the second round of tests and a game plan. You know our daughter: she'll want details."

Mary chuckled. "That she would," she agreed. "Have you told your lady-friend?"

That's what she called Betty. I don't think it was spiteful, I just always thought she had no idea of what else to call her. Girlfriend sounded too juvenile, and we weren't engaged. Perhaps just calling her Betty was too informal for her. "I haven't told anyone, except you. Can't tell Betty until I tell Caroline. She's a cop, remember? She thinks like Caroline."

That actually got a laugh out of her.

There was a few moments of uncomfortable silence, and I knew it was time to hang up. "Thanks for listening, Mary," I said. "I'd probably better be going."

"Corney?" she said hesitantly.

"Yes?"

"You call me. Anytime. I mean it, day or night."

"I will, Mary, if I need to."

"Promise me."

"I promise," I said. "Love you always." That had been our custom since the days before we were married. Just because we weren't married anymore, didn't change things.

"Love you always, too."

We rang off. The day was still beautiful, but my heart felt heavy. I had spoken the words out loud. I probably had cancer. Which meant, even though we hadn't actually said it, we both knew I was probably going to die sooner rather than later.

Oddly enough I felt at peace. Maybe it was the day, maybe it was telling someone else and not carrying the burden all alone. If I was going to die, I was glad I had been given enough notice. I remembered reading somewhere once (probably *Reader's Digest*) that was the only good thing about cancer. It usually took you slow, giving you some time to settle your accounts in the hotel of life before you checked out of your room for good.

I took another look around the park that had given me so many wonderful memories and then headed to my car.

The only stop I made on the way home was to pick up a couple of hitchhikers named Jesse James and The Marlboro Man.

When I arrived at my apartment, the thought of a nap sounded good, but I found that no matter how I tried, I couldn't keep my eyes closed. *One drink*, I told myself. *Just one to ease my nerves.*

One drink turned into nearly one bottle. Eventually I passed out on my sofa.

I woke without a hangover. That was scary in itself. I wondered if I was already starting to get used to getting blind drunk at night. I knew I had to get a hold on my drinking. If I did only have half a year to live, I didn't want to go out stupid drunk. If I was honest, I didn't want to end the same way I'd lived: bland as white bread.

I tallied up my life's accomplishments and came to the grand total of helping to raise a fine young woman up from a child. Nothing to shrug off, but not really what you wanted to see as your only plus grade on St. Peter's scorecard. I wondered if there was enough time to leave a mark behind.

It was Sunday morning. I knew I could go to church. I could call my daughter. I could call Betty.

I went to the grocery store and did my laundry.

Some weeks pass like a whisper on the wind. They're gone before you know it. The following week lumbered like an old man with a club foot on a hundred mile hike. Harvey told me there were complications getting my tests booked. Each day I began, planning to call on either Caroline or Betty, but each night I found other things to do. How could I talk to either of them, when I didn't really know myself?

Finally Friday drug itself around. Harvey called me and wanted to meet at lunch.

"So what's going on with these tests?" I asked over a mouthful of cafeteria baked chicken.

"I'm sorry," he said. "The short version is that I still can't get them booked."

I was angry, but blowing up wouldn't help any. "Harvey," I said, "you gotta help me out here. First you tell me I've only got six months tops if I do nothing, now it's two weeks later and you still haven't begun a plan."

"I know," he said, "and I'm sorry. But we can't move forward until we get the next round of testing to be sure of the seriousness of your condition."

"I'd say six months to live is pretty damn serious."

"That is only my guess in a worst case scenario. I need actual results, you know that."

"So can't we find another place to run the tests?"

"Yes," he admitted. "I will make some calls this afternoon, I give you my word."

Realizing I was transferring my anger onto Harvey, I mentally stepped back. He'd told me the news, he was not *responsible* for the news. "Sorry, Harvey," I said. "I'm just all wound up inside. Sometimes it slips out."

"I know," he said. "No problem. I've got a pretty tough skin. I need one in this business."

Harvey was a good friend as well as my doctor. We'd taken lunch together countless times over the years. Then we'd always talked sports, movies, or music. Not cancer. I made it a point to ask him if he'd seen the Chandler movies on last week. From there it went on, almost, like it always had. At least there was no more talk about the Big C.

I was on my way home when Harvey called. It seemed the kinks in the testing had finally worked out. I was booked a week from this coming Wednesday. That would make it three weeks gone. Nearly a month into my given six, I thought, but didn't say.

By the time I'd gotten home, I was so damned relieved to be moving forward that I didn't feel the need for a drink. I ordered some Chinese to be delivered and fired up my laptop, intending to check my email. Eventually I found myself on the Milford Police Blotter website.

A Susan Applewhite had been reported missing by a friend and co-worker.

I read it again. How damn many Susan Applewhites could there be? I switched over to her Facebook page. A dozen or so of her friends had posted on her timeline, asking if she was okay. A part of me wanted to post that *No, she is not okay, she is dead*, but I knew better.

It was obvious I wasn't going to finish my meal so I lit a cigarette and poured a double. The drink went down pretty smooth, so I poured another.

I was into my third double and second cigarette when I finally called out. "Sister Bertha," I said, flatly. "I'm ready to listen, now."

There was no noise, no creepy fog, no slow dissolve; she just suddenly appeared, sitting across my table as if she'd been there all along. Maybe she had, but I was not ready to see. "It's happening again," she said in that gurgle-croak voice.

"What?"

"Another person will die tonight."

"People die every night," I said, but it was the bourbon talking.

"Not by him," she said. He only takes one and only on a Friday night."

"How do you know all this?" I asked.

"I've talked to the others."

"What others?"

"There's hundreds of them, thousands or maybe more. Those he took before me. We are all in a Purgatory of sorts."

"*Thousands?*"

"Or more."

Lighting another cigarette, I said, "Purgatory, that's like some kind of temporary Hell, right?"

"Close enough."

"But thousands or more? How damn long is temporary?"

"Until he's destroyed."

"Then what happens?"

"We all move on. Until then, we're trapped in this… temporary Hell. Can't go back, can't go on."

"And I'm the only one who can do it?" I asked, pouring another double.

She laughed. It was a disturbing bubbling laugh. Like her mouth was full of blood. "Of course not. You are not that special. It's just that—"

"I've got one foot in each world," I finished for her.

"That and the fact that you know what he is, and you are connected through me."

"Lucky me."

"No, actually I'd say it was damned you." She chuckled at her own joke.

"Where is Susan Applewhite?" I asked.

"Right here." And suddenly she was also sitting at my table.

I glanced at the bottle, finding it near empty. I tipped it up and drained the contents. The room took on a soft fuzzy appearance. It would soon be lights out, experience had taught me. "So just for laughs, let's say I believe this is real," I said when the bottle was empty, "and not my mind falling in on itself. You're saying if I find and destroy this Prophet, you can move on to the next life?"

Sister Bertha nodded. "Not just the two of us," she said. "All of his victims. Some of those poor souls have been waiting a long time."

"Such a deal," I said. I'm not sure if it was the bourbon, the stress of knowing I probably had the same condition that killed my father early, or the fact that I was willingly talking to someone I knew to be dead. Regardless of the reason, I blacked out.

# 5

I woke in the morning stiff from sleeping with my head on the kitchen table. The room was empty, so was the bottle. I wondered if I was losing my mind. People thought they saw things when they didn't all the time. I went to Facebook.

Susan Applewhite's page was still full of posts from friends wondering where she was. I hadn't made that up.

I showered, made coffee and sat down to drink it. Where was this all going? I couldn't exactly run off on some wild goose chase looking for a roadside Prophet who may or may not be killing people. I couldn't exactly call the cops either. Even Betty would have doubts about my sanity if I told her I had been talking with a dead woman and her friend. I certainly couldn't tell her I knew about Susan Applewhite and ask her to find out if the Resurrection Church Tent Revival had made an appearance.

Speaking of which, didn't Sister Bertha say another one was due?

"Sister Bertha?" I called out.

No one appeared in my apartment.

Even if I was losing my mind, I needed food for the week. I got dressed and went out to my car, heading to the grocery store. Maybe I'd check the Redbox for a new movie to watch while I was there.

I was about halfway to the store when I lit my first smoke of the day.

"You do know those things will kill you."

Startled, I glanced into my rearview mirror. Sister Bertha, Susan Applewhite and a middle aged white woman I'd never seen before sat in my backseat.

"Doc, meet Trudy Jackson, formally of Whitehall. Bastard Prophet took her life last night."

"Hello Trudy," I said, looking at the woman. Her throat had been slashed just as Sister Bertha and Susan's were.

"You have to stop this," Sister Bertha said.

"And if I don't?" I asked.

"You need to get a bigger car."

With that, the car was suddenly empty, again.

I drove the rest of the way in silence. I shopped in silence. I wanted to go back home, find a James Cagney movie on Vudu and forget it all. I didn't want to think about a fleabag road show Prophet and dead women.

By the time I'd gotten home and heated the frozen pizza I'd bought for lunch, an idea crossed my mind. I tried to push it back. I didn't want to think about it, but it wouldn't go away.

I accepted that somehow I knew about Susan Applewhite before anything was public knowledge, maybe she commented on one of our mutual friend's page and I noticed the name. It was odd, but not unheard of. There were stories of people who dreamed numbers, played them and won the lottery. I'd just got the other side of the coin. I got the suck side. Instead of winning numbers, I got a vision of someone's death.

*Disappearance*, I told myself. Only a disappearance at this point.

One thing in my life that had always been true was that there was never a pad of notepaper around when I needed one.

While the oven preheated I took the pizza out of the box and then tore a corner from the container. I found a pen and wrote *Trudy Jackson, Whitehall?* on it and then placed it near the laptop along with the day's receipt. It took a day or two before you could report a missing adult. More if you lived alone and had no one to check on you.

A shudder ran through me. My grandmother used to say a goose had walked over her grave as a way of explaining the feeling. Call it what you will, I suddenly realized that it was quite possibly the way I would one day be reported missing. If I died on a Friday night, it might be Monday before I was noticed missing, and maybe Tuesday or Wednesday before anyone came looking for me. I was glad I didn't own a cat.

The weekend passed quietly. I made it a Vudu weekend; watching a lot of my old favorites and making some new ones. I even caught a theater matinee of a new Ben Affleck movie on Sunday. I hadn't been to a movie theater in years. I used to go all the time. I loved the theater, but over the years a trip to the movies left me feeling less than fulfilled anymore. People bring their kids in and let them cry, or talk on the phone, or amongst themselves during the picture. There were just too many distractions anymore. I bought myself a small buttered popcorn in the red and white striped box, another thing I hadn't had in years. I think it was kind of nostalgic for me, given the news rolling around in my subconscious. I'd left the ticket and snack receipts on the pile next to the laptop. Sister Bertha didn't come calling and I stayed away from my laptop. Monday also went smoothly. No visits from dead churchgoers, no excursions to the internet, no thoughts of cancer eating me from the inside out and no chats with Jesse James. I even finished Chandler's *The Big Sleep*. In fact everything went well until just before lunch on

Wednesday. That's when Harvey called and requested to meet me.

"I want you to take tomorrow off," he said over his chef's salad. "I've got you scheduled for your follow-up tests."

"Tomorrow's Thursday," I said. "What happened to next week?"

"I got it bumped up," he told me. "Pulled a few strings."

"I need to take all day?"

"Well the tests are at one o'clock. I guess you could take a half day if you wanted."

I thought about it. "Guess I'll take the day," I said. "What do you think they'll show?"

Harvey gave me a look. "If I knew, I wouldn't have to get you tested."

"I realize that," I said. "I'm just asking you to spitball. As a friend."

My friend put his fork down. He half smiled, but it never reached his eyes. "I don't like it," he finally said. "In fact I'm having these tests done in hopes they prove me wrong."

I found my appetite had left the room. I thanked Harvey for his honesty and went back to the lab. I told Roger I was going home early and wouldn't be in the next day. Shit had just gotten real.

I called Betty on the drive home and told her the news.

"Jesus," she said. "I don't know what to say."

"Nothing much to say," I told her. "At least not until these tests are over and Harvey gets the results. I just wanted you to know, now."

She was silent, wondering no doubt what to say. "Want to get dinner tonight?" she asked."

"I think I'll pass."

"That's what I figured. Just know I'm here. Call me anytime day or night, okay?"

"I promise."

More silence. "You do know I love you," she said.

"I do, and I love you too. We just can't live together."

We shared an uneasy laugh and rang off.

I knew I needed to call Caroline. I even picked up my cell phone a couple of times, found her number, but couldn't bring myself to actually make the call. Not yet, anyway. Instead when I got home I Googled the Whitehall police blotter and discovered a Trudy Jackson had been reported missing since Friday night.

In some ways a Medical Examiner's job is part detective. If the cause of death isn't obvious, like say a slashed throat, it takes a bit of investigation to determine what killed the subject. Someone in their twenties for example with no outward signs of trauma is found dead in their bed, for instance Now the process takes time. It might be a heart attack, a brain aneurism, drug overdose or alcohol poisoning for starters. In those cases we start with what we know and remove all possible options that prove untrue until we are left with what is the truth. Blood work can rule out drugs or alcohol pretty quickly. If they come up negative, we look deeper.

I'd worked on Friday, gone grocery shopping on Saturday and eaten the pizza that evening. The receipt from the grocery store was time stamped at 2:15 pm Saturday. According to Google Maps, Whitehall was way too far away. There was no way I could have left work Friday at five, driven that far, kidnapped a woman and been home to grocery shop by two the next day. I was not the killer.

The second possibility was that I had become a psychic. Sure the world was full of shuck and jive hustlers telling you what you wanted to hear, but there was too much proof that honest people did exist that could *see* things unknown to them. Although I'd never heard of psychic visions suddenly coming to people in their forties.

All that brought me to the last most unbelievable possibility: Sister Bertha was *not* manufactured by my subconscious and she *had* spoken to me from beyond the grave.

I really didn't like that option. But just like my job, sometimes the most unlikely answer was the truth. Sometimes a psychically fit twenty-something person did actually have a heart attack without any advance warning. And sometimes it killed them in the dead of night in their sleep.

Also like my day job, when you didn't like the only answer that fit, the first thing you do is try to disprove it. No one likes the idea of an otherwise healthy young person dying of a heart attack in their sleep. So, you dig deeper—looking for some preexisting circumstance you may have missed.

Of the three possibilities I could think of, seeing (and talking to) a dead woman was my least favorite. I would have preferred to think God gave me a head knocker and a touch of psychic vision, even if it wasn't the winning lottery numbers.

Sister Bertha, I did believe, could have been nothing more than guilt. After all, I didn't see her until after her corpse had shown up on my table. Not to mention the first thing she did was to forgive me for making fun of her when she had been alive. If that didn't sound like guilt four-squared, I didn't know what did. Just a scenario brought on by my mind to deal with the guilt.

If I accepted that Susan Applewhite had been someone on some Facebook post or game I had seen and added a touch of intuition, I could accept it was really just one of those things that happen to everyone now and again. We all get a hunch about something for no reason and when it turns out to be true, we wonder why we couldn't have gotten the lottery numbers instead. Right?

It all seemed possible up to that point. Then Trudy Jackson gets added to the mix and blew my entire theory to Hell. I had never seen or heard the name until Sister Bertha had *introduced* us on Saturday.

Try as I might, I couldn't pigeonhole Sister Bertha into being no more than a visual representation of a psychic hunch. If she started as a guilty conscious, how could she morph into intuition?

Truth was, no matter how much I didn't want to accept it; I had been talking to dead people.

There wasn't much left for me to do that evening. Harvey said I could eat as long as I was finished by seven and no alcohol, period. I wasn't really hungry anyway. He never said anything about cigarettes or coffee before seven. I brewed a cup, got my smokes and sat down.

Firing up the first Marlboro of the day I called out, "Okay Sister Bertha. I think I'm ready to really listen, now."

I sat, smoking and waiting. After two cigarettes and a full cup of coffee I was ready to say the hell with the whole thing. What was I trying to prove? That I could summon the dead on command? I snubbed the smoke in the ashtray. "Maybe I am crazy," I said, feeling a little more than a bit foolish.

And she was sitting across from me at my table.

I had thought I was prepared for Sister Berta to appear. I wasn't prepared for her actual appearance. Gone was the smooth skinned blonde woman I'd seen at the tent revival. The flesh of the woman who sat across from me was bloated and decomposing. Startled, I sucked in some air.

"Not pretty, huh?" she asked, in that gurgling voice.

"What happened to you?" I asked.

"I was murdered, remember?"

"Yeah, but you didn't look like this before."

"Before you didn't believe. Now you do. I've been dead almost a month. Given your profession, you above all people know what an over three week old dead body looks like."

It made sense in its own way. I'd had seen worse bodies on the job. Of course those didn't actually talk to me.

"Where were you?" I asked. "I've been waiting for twenty minutes."

"Making sure you were serious," she said. "I had my doubts about you. Besides, after blowing me off and fainting on the floor, I wanted to see you sweat a little bit."

"Great," I said. "Of all the dead people in the world, I get one with an attitude."

She smiled. "You were expecting the likes of a Patrick Swayze?"

I don't think I'd ever wanted a drink as bad as I did those next two hours. There's just something about chatting with a decomposing corpse as natural as if she was your next door neighbor talking to you in the hall about the weather. The only good thing was that Sister's Bertha's condition was only a visual. The gut wrenching stench that would accompany a decomposing corpse was nonexistent.

According to Sister Bertha, this Prophet, this thing from the depths of Hell had been doing this for decades, centuries even. He had been draining the life forms of his victims to preserve his own life on the average of once a week. He kept to the shadows, remaining unknown to all around him except his one helper. Currently it was the ragged Carney looking man I'd seen, but there had been countless more before him.

"He keeps their service by healing them of an ailment," she explained, "and promising to grant them everlasting life as well." She smiled. "But that doesn't happen. From what those who came before me told me, he keeps them for a year or so, until he's found a replacement, then he drains them. Can't expect to deal with a devil and get a fair shake."

"What do you mean, 'heal' them?"

"Well, *heal* might not be the right word. It's more like he puts your ailment in a cocoon. Let's say you have a slipped disc in your back: If he wanted he could take all that pain away. If you got x-rayed it wouldn't show. You'd still have a slipped disc, but you wouldn't feel it and you couldn't prove it. You'd feel *healed*, but it was still there, unseen, lurking inside you. In that way he is sort of a Resurrection Man. He doesn't actually raise the dead, but he makes you *feel* as if you have a new lease on life.

"That first night you saw me, I had been suffering from a chronic backache for the past ten years. When he touched my hand, it simply vanished. I think it's what brings people back the next night, bringing their friends."

"And you?"

"I came back alone," she admitted. "That's why he took me that night. No witnesses."

According to her, there were a lot of people like her: Stuck between worlds. Once he took you, it seemed he kept you. He'd managed to go undetected for so long because he stayed on the move and culled his victims cautiously. According to Sister Bertha he had bodies buried all over the country. It was only a fluke that Bertha and I were connected. She was sure it was because of the cancer. As far as she was concerned, Harvey's follow up tests were a waste of time. I had cancer and I was dying. She knew this without a doubt. "A foot in both worlds," she told me again.

Even though she could converse of sorts with those before her and with those behind, she had no idea where the demon was at any time.

"I was kind of hoping you could put me on the trail."

"Sorry," she said. "Where he was I know, where he's going is blind to me."

"So exactly what do you expect me to do?"

"Find him and destroy him. His body is flesh. He's a soulless creature, but flesh does bleed."

"And if he bleeds, he can die?"

"Exactly," she said tiredly.

"Are you okay?"

"No," she said with a weak smile. "I'm dead and I can't move on."

I looked closer at her. Her eyes were sunken. True enough, she was looking all of three weeks dead, except for her eyes. Her eyes look like someone who'd been burning the candle at both ends too long: alive, but exhausted. They hadn't looked that way earlier. "Very funny," I said. "What is the problem?"

"It takes a lot of," she paused, looking for the word, "*energy* to come to you and we've been talking for nearly two hours. I think I need to go now. I can come back tomorrow if you want."

That feeling of guilt you get when you know you've caused someone else pain flooded through me. "Okay," I said. "Let's talk tomorrow."

She was gone as quickly as she had arrived.

Truth was I didn't know what to think. I've always been open minded when it came to life beyond this one. If you've ever asked a true believer how they can accept the existence of God when they can't see Him, chances are they asked you how you can believe in air when you can't see it. If you told them it was because you breathed air, felt it in your lungs, they'd probably countered with it's the same way with God. You feel Him. I grew up in the church, but distanced myself from it, but never quite turned my back on the Almighty. I've often wondered how any rational person could argue for certainty there is or isn't a God. I always figured it was up to each person how they felt.

But there were things going on I could not understand. I did what I had done since Med School. I got out some paper and a pen, and then sat down at the table to puzzle it out. There was a teacher in my first year of school who often quoted Sir Arthur Conan Doyle's *Sherlock Holmes*. She was fond of reminding the class according to Holmes, "When you have eliminated the impossible, whatever remains, no matter how improbable, must be the truth." I never forgot those words. Damned if I could remember which book they'd been written in, though. I modified it by adapting the motto that when dealing with something that made no sense, you wrote down the facts, possible explanations, (no matter how farfetched they seemed) and then worked it until you were satisfied. The result may not be THE truth, but it was *your* truth.

Mine looked like this:

I HAVE CANCER.

My father had it and it killed him. Genetically I had always been predisposed to getting it myself. That is why I got tested every year since I'd turned twenty-five. I've always known it would come looking for me, I just wanted a heads up when it arrived. Harvey could tell me all day he had only wanted another round of tests to be sure of the original result, but I knew better. He wanted the tests to see how much of me had already been eaten alive from the inside. That and to help form a game plan for keeping me alive a little longer.

Knowing the Big C had finally found me, had opened my mind up to a host of things I hadn't previously thought of. Most of all, how little I'd accomplished in my allotted time, so far. Sort of a midlife crisis and life's end.

I KNEW ABOUT PEOPLE WHO VANISHED BEFORE THEY WERE REPORTED.

That was a fact. The question was, how?

SISTER BERTHA TOLD ME.

Another fact as far as it went. The real question was,

WHO IS SISTER BERTHA?

I had to accept that it was at least possible that she was who she said she was.

Another possibility of course was that she was a manifestation of my mind, trying to make sense of this sudden intuition about people I didn't know. Honestly I knew nothing more than these women had been reported missing after I already knew about it. I did not know if they were dead or runaway wives. If they were dead, I still didn't know how. I knew Bertha's throat had been slashed and she'd been bled out because I'd seen her body. But were they all bled out just because she told me so, or because my mind made them look that way to me?

People went missing every day. Not many of them were slashed across the throat and bled out like a deer hung on a tree. Maybe I was adding that bit myself, trying to fit the knowledge of their disappearances into the bizarre puzzle of my mind somehow knowing these things. I had read somewhere that even the best of psychics didn't see everything. Somewhere I had read that Nostradamus was wrong more than he was right. It was only the direct hits we actually cared about.

The end result was that I accepted I somehow knew of the disappearances of these women before they were reported. It was impossible for me to be responsible because the distance was too far. Either they were killed by this demented Prophet and his tent show, or they weren't. If they weren't and they weren't connected, why was I getting the knowledge on them?

I didn't have an answer, which meant for now at least, I accepted they were somehow all connected to the Resurrection Church Tent Revival. Bertha had been real in life. She may or may not be real, but my mind said she was. So I accepted it. Somehow I was the only one capable of figuring out the mystery. It was improbable, but as I had already eliminated the impossible, whatever was left, no matter how improbable, had be the truth. At least it was *my* truth.

Which brought me back to cancer. If it had me, and I had no doubt it did, I was going to die sooner rather than later. I could take the treatments and possibly postpone the inevitable, but not for all that long. Survival chances are good with prostate cancer if caught early, but Harvey seemed to think that wasn't my case. Somehow my results went from zero a year ago to death knocking on my door. Even given the medical advances since my father's death, cancer was a stubborn mule headed bitch, and it always won in the end.

I still remember some of the last words my father had ever told me. It was right after what turned out to be his last chemo treatment. They always left him weak and tired. I was standing near his bed; a little boy looking to his father for a promise of a brighter future. But my father was a dying man who finally allowed himself to feel cheated and angry at God.

"Are you going to get better?" I had asked.

He smiled, weakly. "I will try," he said. "And I hope so, but Corney, right now there is not much fun in my life."

Probably not the best thing to say to a little boy

\*\*\*

I looked at my own life. Fun hadn't really been in the equation for more years than I could remember. Wasted time was there, but that was all. Now in what might be my last quarter mile, I wasn't even worried about fun. I was more concerned with leaving something behind. Not money, something worthwhile. I had lived such a complacent life. For the most part in the company of Turner Classic Movie Chanel and my books. Living life vicariously through the adventures of fictional people created by writers. My nice little *safe* life. Never lived on the edge, and what had that gotten me? Nothing.

    A plan began to form in my mind. I had a month's worth of vacation time coming to me. Seemed a shame to die and leave it behind. Even so, I decided it seemed better to sleep on it. After a lifetime of playing it safe, it was kinda hard to simply hold my breath and jump into the water without looking around first.

## 6

*Cansssssser.* The word drifted though my sleeping brain like ground fog in the early morning, the middle sounding like the hiss of a snake. I woke part-way, listening for the sound again. Hearing nothing but the silence of the night, I dozed off again.

*Canssssser.*

My eyes popped open. Floating in the air, arms outstretched and looking like a seedy copy of the Christ the Redeemer statue in Rio de Janeiro, was the road show Prophet from The Resurrection Church Tent Revival. My mouth opened, but no sound came out. He looked at me. "Come unto *meee*," he said. "I will *heeeel* thou."

I opened my eyes and sat straight up in the bed. The Resurrection Church Tent Revival Prophet was gone. Feeling my heart hammering in my chest, I tried to steady my nerves. *A dream within a dream?*

It only took a few moments to put two and two together. Sister Bertha had said, he was a healer of sorts and that her chronic back pain had vanished after his touch. I had a terminal illness. After conventional treatments have been tried and proven unsuccessful, many people take that next step. They try experimental drugs, go see faith healers, ingest natural and unnatural concoctions that have not been tested by the FDA—

anything to try and prolong their death sentence. My subconscious was trying to do the same by bringing that sleazy creature into my dreams offering a healing.

I might have tried it too, except Sister Bertha also said he was killing people to survive. If it all were true, I could beat cancer's ass. All I had to do was turn my back on the murder of innocents.

A look at the clock told me I'd been asleep only a couple hours. "Piss off," I told the silent apartment and went back to sleep.

My sleep was haunted by dreams of the Prophet standing in a darkened room full of cardboard boxes. His hair was disheveled, his robe ratty and his face pure hatred. He tore into each box, removed a stack of papers from within and glanced over them before throwing them into the air. I think he was cursing. At one point I remember the dream shifted to the Christmas I bought Caroline a bicycle when she was five. Her first Christmas with her Mom and Dad not living together. It had been a hot pink thing with training wheels, a flowered white basket on the front and pink and white streamers on the handlebar grips. It was glorious. Living in California as I do, she could ride it Christmas day. She rode that thing every day until she had to return to her mom's. Caroline begged me to let her take it home, and I did. Never did see that bike again. It still hurt when I thought about it. I think it was heartache that woke me.

I found myself covered in sweat, my heart pounding, and I felt strangely violated. It all seemed so odd. I tried closing my eyes again, but sleep would not come. Every time I felt myself drifting off, the vision of that bastard and the cardboard boxes came flooding in again and my heart hammered so hard I opened my eyes. Maybe I needed a drink… or three.

"He's trying to learn your name," Sister Bertha's voice came softly from the dark.

I didn't turn the light on. I really didn't want to see her decomposing flesh. "How's that?"

He wasn't randomly going through paperwork in boxes," she explained. "That was the memories stored in your head. He's looking for your name."

"So my memories are kept on papers shoved into cardboard boxes and stored in a dusty old attic in my brain?"

"It's how your mind chose to show you. It could have been a diary, a collection of canned goods, anything. It was your mind telling you that he's looking through your memories."

"While I'm sleeping."

"It's the only time he can slip in without you stopping him."

"What about Caroline's bike?"

"A particularly strong memory. Strong enough to snap you out of it."

"Why me? Why now?"

"You believe now," she said. "Somehow he knows that, and it scares him. He can feel you, but he doesn't know who you are."

"And that scares him?"

"Yes. He wants to kill you, because you are now a threat to him. He promised to heal you, didn't he? When that didn't work, he went digging."

"How do you know all this?" I asked.

She gave a soft laugh. It was an odd sound, given the slit in her throat. Even so it wasn't completely unpleasant. "We're kinda connected, you know?"

"So I can't sleep anymore?"

There was a pause. "Honestly? I don't know. I'm new at this, but I think it's because he's only awake after dark. He sleeps in the day."

"So I can sleep during the daylight hours?"

"Maybe. I'm just guessing here."

"Does he know about you?" I asked her.

"No. He can only sense that someone has figured out what he is. Who I was, or you are, or even where you are is unknown to him, I think."

"Okay," I told her and closed my eyes, "I'll think about it in the morning."

The dream came back, of course. I think I knew it would. But now, thanks to Sister Bertha, I knew I was dreaming. I stood as the unseen eye of God, watching the "Prophet" tear into the boxes, rip his way through stacks of paper, all the while cussing up a storm. Every now and then, he'd find a memory that flashed through my brain: There were a lot of childhood memories, mostly good, but a lot of my Dad passing as well. Mary and our wedding, the birth of Caroline. A ton of stuff, but nothing with my name on it. I watched all of it with a strange humor, unseen by him.

Until he opened the box with my medical school memories. Then I remembered my diploma. That had my name on it. Even in my sleep I felt the panic begin to rise.

"HEY!" I yelled.

He actually looked up, startled, seeing me for the first time.

"Get out of my head, asshole!"

"I think not," he said. "Why should I? I like it here."

There was something just a bit too cool, too composed to sound right. He was afraid of me. "I don't think so," I said. "I think you're scared of me. Maybe scared of someone for the first time in your history."

"I'll eat your soul," he said. "After I rip out your heart and eat it before your eyes, then pluck out one eye and eat it while you watch with the other." A long graveyard worm tongue that was split into a V wiggled out of his lips and slid up into his nose. After a moment it came back out and shot four feet across the room towards me, both ends of the split writhing in opposite directions.

"Eat my soul? Really? You think quoting *The Evil Dead* is going to frighten me? Really? That the best you got?"

His eyes burned cherry red. His face twisted then actually began to melt. I watched his left eyeball drool out of its socket and slowly stretch down to the floor in a white mucus hanging snot trail. "Looks like bad CGI from a low budget horror movie," I said.

The Prophet screamed at me. His mouth opened in a gaping hole that filled his entire head. Two rows of razor sharp teeth and that graveyard worm tongue. Rancid wind flowed over me, sour enough to turn my stomach. The scream went on for several seconds. I felt like my eardrums were going to explode.

And then he was gone.

And I sat up, awake in my bed. "Piss on it," I mumbled as I got up to make coffee. There would be no more sleep tonight. I stopped by the bathroom to relieve myself; thankful it hadn't frightened me *that* much, and splashed water on my face after washing my hands. As the cold water shocked my skin, the reality of what was happening to me sunk in and pissed me off.

I returned to my bed once more. This time while lying in the dark I thought of that storage room. It really was a good representation of how my life was. Cramming memories into cardboard boxes to maybe look at later. Never once considering that someone might come snooping around. I drew a breath, closed my eyes and calmed my spirit.

There in the quiet of my bedroom the room came into vision behind my eyes. A sad dusty room that was not much more than an attic contained my life. I saw the boxes stacked haphazardly around the floor and decided to make a change. It was *my* room, *my* memories, and I could store them as I wanted to.

First of all, I wanted the boxes to be made of something stronger than cardboard. I looked around the room and the cardboard boxes were gone, replaced by steel boxes with hinged lids. That still wouldn't keep anyone out. Suddenly the steel boxes were wrapped in silver chains, each held secured by a large padlock. The locks were large with a keyhole in the front like something out of the old west. Looking down at my hands I saw that I held a very large ring with a multitude of keys hanging from it. Like an old time sheriff.

I hadn't even realized I'd fallen asleep until *he* showed up. One moment I was admiring the strongboxes I'd secured my memories in, and the next the Prophet was standing in the room. He scowled at the boxes. Walking over to one, he picked it up and yanked on the padlock. It refused to give way. Cussing, the Prophet threw the box across the room and grabbed another. He held the lock in one hand, raised the box over his head and began to slam it repeatedly against the box below it. Still the padlock did not give. I felt myself smiling as his face twisted in rage. He spewed out a solid stream of obscenities as each slam brought no results. From what I saw, the boxes themselves didn't even dent or scratch.

For a moment I wished I'd made the boxes charged with electricity. The Prophet threw the box across the room and grabbed another. Sparks flew into the air as the ozone crackled in the room. The force of the electric shock sent the Prophet backwards through the air and landed him on his ass. His eyes bulged out in pain; his mouth continued their flow of obscenities. I about busted a gut laughing.

It occurred to me that the creature didn't even know I was there. Then it hit me: *My dream, my rules*. He might be a blood drinking, soul trapping demon from Hell itself, but he was powerless over my rules if I refused to fear him.

He continued to pick up, shake and throw the strongboxes across the room. Every time he grabbed a box sparks flew. His hair was a frazzled mess, giving him that Don King look. Yet he continued to look for an open container. Testing my theory about my dream my rules, I concentrated on what I believed would be his next box.

Sure enough, he grabbed the box I had been looking at. Sparks flew, but this time the lid flew open and liquefied horse shit flew out in a gusher, covering his head and face. The Prophet's head tipped back, his mouth stretched out exposing those two rows of pointed teeth and a howl bellowed forth into the room.

"Having fun?" I asked.

His head snapped around, his eyes as red as hot coals glared at me. "Open these damned boxes!" he demanded.

"Don't think so," I said. "Having too much fun watching you."

His neck stretched like that guy in the Fantastic Four as his head sailed across the room, bringing his face inches from my own. His mouth gapped open like a festering sore revealing those two rows of teeth while that split tongue waggled at me, slobber filling the air, yet never touching me. Two extra sets of arms appeared on each side of his body and six clawed hands came at me, stopping just short of actually touching me.

"*You will not fight?*" he hissed.

"I will not *fear*," I said.

His body appendages withdrew back to his torso. His form drew in upon itself until it was nothing more than a red glowing coal suspended in mid air. *"Canssssssser,"* his fading voice filled the air. And then with a loud POP, the room was empty.

I awoke an hour before my alarm went off feeling refreshed, surprisingly enough. I had hours to fill before those damned tests. Hours before I would be able to have my first cup of coffee, I brought the laptop to life and began routing a map beginning with where I first saw the Resurrection Church Tent Revival, on a small side road near East Sacramento, next I plotted out the area where Susan Applewhite died, some three hundred miles North East of there. Trudy Jackson was another couple hundred miles South East from there. The points were jagged, up and down like a jack-o-lantern's mouth. Running between the extreme north and south points ran the old U.S Route 50 which runs between California and Maryland. Three thousand direct miles, parts of which were known as "The Loneliest Road in America," as it runs through a lot of desert, mountains and a lot of farmland as well. Utilizing the far reaching zigzag motion it seemed like it would be weeks before they even got out of California.

It only took a minute to find my bookmark for the single review of The Resurrection Church Tent Revival. The author stated the Revival had appeared just outside of Bridgeport, West Virginia: Also on the U.S. Route 50 run.

I had him.

Well, not really, but I knew the general direction he was heading.

Sort of.

I did some crosschecking between Bertha, Susan and Trudy. The distance was a several hundred miles between each, but nothing carved in stone. The only constant was that Route 50 ran between locations and that the women went missing from the second service on Friday nights. That made me believe that they drove on an angle for a few hundred miles until probably Wednesday. They weren't pulling permits for the gathering, so they'd want to put up signs not any earlier than Thursday morning to catch the eyes of area road travelers. By Friday night they'd have their last area show, gotten the Prophet's blood sacrifice, pulled up the signs and moved on into the night.

The wild card was deciding *where* they would set up shop. In all three of the locations I had, it was rural areas with little else going for them. That gave me something to pinpoint my direction on. I plotted a course between two and three hundred miles North East of Trudy Jackson's last known whereabouts, looking for small rural areas that fit my idea.

It took about an hour to pull in every small town within a three hundred mile radius of where I thought the next Revival might take place. It wasn't much. It wasn't anything, really. Just a possible killing field for some saddened person looking for a miracle in this tough life and finding only death and damnation.

A quick check of the time showed I still had a few hours before my follow up tests. Looking at the whole picture it seemed nothing short of ludicrous. I had cancer. Harvey had pretty much told me so. The follow up tests were only to decided how long I'd live, not *if* I'd live, no matter how much Harvey tried to sugarcoat them. Eventually cancer always won, given enough time. And yet, someone within my mapped area would be taken hostage, bled out, and their body unceremoniously dumped in a shallow grave somewhere. Their remaining years having been stolen from them by some soulless creature from Hell.

I called Roger and told him I'd be using all my four weeks of vacation right then. After that I hung up and went to pack my bags.

Not on my watch.

Looking back on it now, I think it was knowing I had cancer that suddenly turned me, a quiet unassuming man, into what I'd become. Cancer does stuff to a lot of people. Seems everybody knows at least one person who has beat cancer into remission and the next thing you know, they're partying all night, having affairs and such. It's as if facing cancer down pushed them to life on the edge afterward. Grabbing all the gusto in life, so to speak, as if life was ending the middle of the next week. Not everyone, of course, but I'd be willing to bet if a study was done, a good many marriages went south within a year of one spouse beating cancer to sleep.

That's the only reason I have found to justify my sudden urge to leave my quiet life and go balls to the wall on what I never before would have even believed possible. Let's be honest: Looking back it sounds like I was a madman on a hell bent quest over a nonexistent demon. And maybe I was… a madman at least.

A long time ago I began putting together a bankroll of money hidden in my apartment. We may live in a plastic world, but I've never really trusted it. Over the years I built up the amount to five thousand dollars in cash. After a moment of consideration, I put the five stacks of twenty dollar bills in the suitcase between my underwear and my socks. I wasn't sure what I was going to do, but felt it was probably best I didn't leave an electronic paper trail with a plastic card. As I was throwing the rest of my things into my suitcase and a backpack, one thing kept bothering me. If the Prophet could look into my mind as I slept, a passageway must have been opened. If there was a passage between our minds, couldn't I use it too? Bertha had said he slept during the day. If I'm to be honest, I didn't really know if I wanted to see into his memories. If this creature had been on the loose for as long as Bertha thought, God alone knew what horrors waited in his memories. How many innocent deaths would I find? The memory of Sister Bertha's slit throat ran through my mind. Would I be forced to witness that and others? I really didn't know if I could face that orgy of bloodletting. No, that's not true. I knew damn well I wanted no part of it.

But, the belief that I might just save a life and countless lives to come if I destroyed the bastard now, made the decision for me. When I had packed everything I thought I'd need, I laid down on my bed. Inside I was way too jittery to actually fall asleep, but I forced myself to close my eyes. Breathing deep I pictured the room I stored my memory boxes in.

Breath in.
Breath out.
Breath in.
Breath out.

And I was there. Even though I knew I was dreaming, it was as real as anything I had ever experienced. Dimly lit room, with the yellow glow of the single hanging light bulb, the bare wood walls and rafters that smelled old and dank, like some long forgotten attic. The boxes were still secured as they had been. The room piled high with them. Across the room I saw a door I didn't remember seeing before, but I knew my dreamworld had added it.

Drawing a deep breath, I walked straight to the door. It was unlocked. I drew another breath, holding it in against what I feared might be on the other side and opened it.

On the other side of the door a red tinted wasteland greeted me. Sand the color of dried blood stretched on seemingly endlessly until it reached the lighter fresh blood red colored skyline. Above it all heat lightning flashed filling the air with an ozone smell. Melancholy engulfed my soul and wrapped my heart in battleship chains.

That was it; *emptiness*, plain and simple. A complete vacuum of memories and emotions. According to Sister Bertha the bastard had been slaughtering innocent people for a very long time, and he had NO memories? No remorse? No thoughts at all on the spilled blood he'd left in his wake?

Chain lightning, white hot against the red sky, continued to flash on the horizon. I felt the hair on my arms stand up with the sizzle and scent of ozone. The thunder that followed shook all the way back to the doorway I was standing in. The desert sand began to ripple in waves. I knew he knew I was there.

I stepped back into my memory room and closed the door.

When I woke, Sister Bertha was standing at my bedside. "What are you going to do?" she asked.

"I'm going to rip the lid off Hell and toss him back where he came from," I told her.

"Good," she said, and vanished.

Still lying on my bed ten minutes later, I continued to feel the tremors of anger inside me This creature, this self proclaimed *prophet*, thought so little of humans as to not even retain a single memory? The taking of human life was no more than sustenance to him. The lives taken, the lives destroyed, the trust in what this sonofabitch claimed to be—all nothing in his eyes. No more emotion than we would have eating a cheese puff snack. There was something about that truth that made it worse than the lives taken. It was downright insulting and that somehow made it all even more obscene.

To top matters off, my damned eyes began to itch. In fact it felt like someone had poured itching powder from my eyeballs clear back into my brain. I lay there staring at the ceiling scratching my head and temples feverishly to no avail. The itch wasn't on my scalp; it felt like the contents of an anthill had been emptied *inside* my head. Like two hundred tiny little red ants were crawling madly about between my skull and the gray matter of my brain. My eyes felt no better. It was as if they too had ants scurrying across them. I closed my eyes and rubbed the lids viciously, as if to squash the unseen insects, but to no avail.

The itching went from scurrying ants to barbed fishhooks sunk deep within my brain in a matter of minutes. A scream welled up inside me as I felt my brain being ripped apart from every different angle possible. But, before the sound could reach the outside air, the pain vanished.

I lay there in bed, eyes closed, trying to regain control of my breathing. I had the strangest desire to get up and find my wallet. Not only that, but to take my driver's license out and look at it. It was as if I needed to look at the information, to make sure my name and the address were properly reported.

*Why?*

Fighting the urge, I continued to lay still with my eyes closed. Why did I want to look at my driver's license of all things, and why now?

Because it wasn't really my desire at all. Lying still, I began to feel as if I was no longer alone. Not in the room, but inside my head. It was almost as if I was a tourist in my own mind. As if someone else was looking for something.

The Prophet.

Somehow by entering his memory room, I must have left a trail back to my conscious mind. Why else would I want to see my name and address on my license? Because he still didn't know who I was. The words of Sister Bertha came back to me: *"You believe now. Somehow he knows that, and it scares him. He can feel you, but he doesn't know who you are."*

It made sense to me.

The bastard had followed me back into my head. He was the one wanting to see my driver's license. It might have scared me. It probably should have scared me. But at that moment the only emotion I was feeling was anger. Simple blood boiling, wounded animal backed into a corner, personally violated, PISSED OFF.

"Get the hell outta my mind!" I yelled and snapped my eyes closed.

"Nope," I said aloud to the empty room. "Not going to happen."

I could feel him, and he *was* scared. Always used to getting what he wanted. Never challenged. Never known.

"This is my life," I said. "MINE. Do you hear me?"

Nothing. He was playing possum.

"This my life," I said again, "and you are not welcome. BE GONE!"

For the briefest of moments I thought my brain had exploded into gray mush inside my skull. Then, nothing except for the ceiling fan overhead in my room and my own ragged breathing.

"Well, I'll be damned," I told the empty room. "Or not."

It took some time but I finally got my breathing under control. The entire time I lay there with my eyes closed, I searched inside myself for any outside influences. There was nothing to find. I was truly alone with myself. The Prophet was gone.

The one thought that did gnaw at my soul was not how he had gained access into my head. That didn't matter. He was there and I threw him out. I had a feeling that if I'd allowed myself to actually be scared rather than pissed off, he would have won. Perhaps fear itself really is all we should fear.

The one question that remained was that if he could find a way into my head—why couldn't I find one into his? Given the terrible emotions that consumed me witnessing the barrenness of his lack of memories or conscious, did I really want to creep around in his mind?

No, I surely did not. However, the possibility of looking through his eyes was another story. If I could see what he was seeing, maybe I could pinpoint his location.

A long shot to be sure. Then again, what else was I running on anyway?

Glancing at the alarm clock on my nightstand I saw it was nearly three in the afternoon. I'd slept a lot longer than I'd expected and I had missed my appointment. Harvey would be pissed. I got up and grabbed my packed bags. I wasn't too sure of my final destination, but I had miles of Route 50 highway before I even got close to the general area I thought might be the next location of The Resurrection Church Tent Revival. If my theory was right the Prophet and his Carney sidekick should be getting ready for their Thursday night performance at their newest hunting grounds in three or four hours.

After throwing my bags into the trunk, I ran a mental checklist and returned inside for my laptop. As I locked the door, I had a moment of what you might call sanity, and wondered what the hell I was doing. Then, before I could question myself, I got in the car and headed for Route 50 Eastbound. The gas gage read at half full, but as I have a Kia Soul, that meant I could be beyond the point of no return before I needed to pull over for more fuel. At an average of sixty miles per hour I figured with a few needed breaks, I could be in the area somewhere after midnight, if I could actually drive that long. I'd never make the tonight's service, but if I could locate where they were set up, I could be in attendance for the final Friday service. The night the Prophet would be picking his next meal.

I fired up the Soul and dropped into reverse. I needed some fighting music to drive by. After a moment I located my Dropkick Murphys CD, slid it in and the opening strains to *Hang 'Em High* filled the car. *That* was exactly what I planned to do with both the Prophet and his Carney sidekick. The irony of the second song being titled, *Going Out In Style*, was not lost to me. In a way, it was perfect. As far off of center that my mind told me my actions were, I had made the commitment. I would succeed, or I would go out in style.

There were just too many questions I had no answers for. Like how did I actually expect to kill something that had been alive for centuries? So I drove on and rocked on, hoping my subconscious would find an answer to that.

I drove that way for nearly four hours; blasting some kickass rock music and singing at the top of my lungs. I'd always been a good singer. Alone. With no witnesses. Once, when we were first married Mary talked me into trying Karaoke at a local bar. When I heard the playback, my days of public singing were forever over. I can't carry a tune in a bucket with both hands. In the car alone, however, it is a different story. I am a rock star in the car.

It was nearing six-fifteen and I was belting out my rendition of The Rolling Stones, *Jumpin' Jack Flash* when Sister Bertha appeared in my passenger seat, scaring the crap out of me. "He'll begin soon," she said.

"I know," I told her, glancing across the car. I was surprised at what I saw. "You don't look so good," I told her.

"I'm dead," she said. "I've been dead awhile."

"Things you never thought you'd hear from someone riding in your passenger seat," I said. "Seriously, you don't look…" I paused, searching for the right phrase. "You don't look…"

"I'm weak," she said. "Being that this my first time dead, I don't understand it, but that's how it feels."

"Okay," I told her. "I'm glad you're here. Something happened I wanted to tell you about."

I spent the next fifteen minutes explaining the invasion in my brain earlier. I told her of the itching that turned into a thousand scurrying ants running across my brain, that turned into barbed fishhooks sunk into the grey matter and then being yanked out from all sides feeling as if my entire brain was being ripped apart inside my skull. I explained my sudden urge to get my driver's license out and look at it. "Now why would I want to do that?" I asked. "It makes no sense."

"It was him," she said simply.

"That's what I felt," I told her. "Can he do that? Can he enter my head, look through my eyes and make me look at things he wants?"

"He invaded your memories, didn't he?"

"Yeah, he did. And I invaded his, such as they were. Do you think I could look through his eyes?"

"He opened a path between your memories and you followed it back to his," she said. "Seems logical if he's opened a path to your eyes, you should be able to follow that back as well."

The thought of entering that Hellborn mind scared the crap out of me. There was no way I wanted to do it. I didn't want to take a chance for fear of what, I didn't know. I just didn't want to do it, but I would. I knew that.

But the idea of doing so while driving, or even on the side of the highway, wasn't at all appealing. I needed to get a room.

As in answer to a prayer, the lights of a Motel 6 came into view ahead on the left. I noticed a diner called Tippy's across the street from the motel. It was then my stomach reminded me I hadn't actually eaten all day. I hit the directional and pulled into the parking lot.

"What are you doing?" Sister Bertha asked.

"I have an idea," I said, pulling the car up to the office.

## 7

One benefit of having an invisible friend is the fact that you only need to pay for a single room, or a single meal, I thought as I walked out of Tippy's Diner back across the street to my room.

I opened the door expecting to see Sister Bertha, but the room was empty. Unsure what to do next, I sat the Styrofoam container of Tippy's Cheeseburger Deluxe with a side order of crispy fries on the table by the window and took a seat on the bed.

With my eyes closed I began deep breathing, trying to center myself. It was ten to eight and the Prophet would be knee deep in his sermon about healing and miracles. Hopefully too engrossed to notice if I came peeking in. It wasn't easy, my mind was buzzing with a million distractions, making concentration near impossible. Finally I imagined the color red being all I could see behind my closed eyelids. With each exhale, I imagined the red shrinking a little, revealing the blackness behind it. My heartbeat slowed down, a fact I was marginally aware of.

Finally the red shrunk to nothing more than the cherry head of a burning cigarette in a pitch black room, and then that too was gone.

*My Lawd doesn't want you in pain!*

The voice in my brain sounded like it came from under water.

*My Lawd wants you whole again!*

The voice became clearer and louder.

The blackness began to lighten, replaced by a vision of people seated in folding chairs under a tent.

*No benevolent God would want you sick, hurt or impaired in any way!*

The voice got clearer as did the vision of those seated beneath the tent.

*That is not my God! That is the other, the one who forces you to suffer!*

The Prophet bellowed and I was there.

I was actually inside, looking through *his* eyes. He stopped abruptly, feeling my presence. Without hesitation I turned my head-his head, to look out, past the tent at the horizon. A field. A barn with what looked like a time faded ad for Barbasol Shaving Cream painted on the tin roof came into view.

Emotions began filling my brain. I felt outrage, I felt anger and best of all I felt *fear*.

The Prophet raised his hands—our hands—before our eyes and slowly balled his fingers against our palms, turning them into fists. I felt the fingernails biting into our palms. Felt the blood ooze out from the meat of our palms. I felt our breath being squeezed from our lungs—*my* lungs.

The tent revival went blurry, then fuzzy, then blackness overtook me.

When I came back around Sister Bertha was there, hovering over me. Only she didn't look like the decomposing corpse anymore. She looked like she had on that first tent revival. "Did you do it?" she asked.

The world was still blurry around me, and my throat felt raw. "Water," I managed to say. "Need water."

"*Really?*" she said. "You expect me to get it for you?"

The knowledge that she wasn't really there, she was dead, a spirit at best, came back to me. "Sorry," I said. "Got confused. You look… better… now." My voice was still cracking.

"Yeah, well, I pushed a little harder. Didn't think you needed to wake up to my real face," she said. "But you'll have to get your own damn water. I can't do anything physical in the real world anymore." Her voice was calm and understanding.

Glancing at my watch I saw it was past nine. "Sorry," I said, forcing myself to stand up and strip off my clothes. Using the wall, I made my way into the bathroom and turned on the shower. Memories of those last few moments still clawed at the back of my mind.

It only took a few minutes under the cold water to blast through the haze in my brain and have me firing on all cylinders again. As my brain began to clear I tipped my head back and drank from the cool water splashing down across my face. My throat began to feel better. Slowly the feeling of my lungs being crushed faded away. As those memories dimmed, the memory of my last vision in the Prophet's eyes came front and center.

When I stepped from the shower, I had, for the first time, a plan. As I got dressed I told Sister Bertha what I had experienced.

She looked at me, her face once again shrunken, the skin drawn tight in dehydration and decomposition with patches of blue forming on her dead flesh. (Oddly enough, although I did notice, it didn't bother me.) "Outrage, anger and fear?" she asked.

I nodded.

She smiled. It would have looked gruesome to most people; a grinning corpse. But I understood just fine. "You have him worried. I doubt he's ever been invaded before."

"You need to eat," she added, pointing at the take-out container from Tippy's.

I looked at my watch; it was just past nine. "I'll be right back," I told her heading outside. When I returned a few minutes later with my laptop and a can of Coke from the vending machine outside the office, I sat down at the little table and connected to the Wi-Fi.

"What are you doing?" she asked.

"Looking for Barbasol Shaving Cream," I told her around a mouthful of cold Cheeseburger Deluxe.

It took nearly half an hour, one cold Cheeseburger Deluxe and a cold order of fries before I found what I was looking for. As wonderful as the internet is, looking for some small bit of information when you have next to nothing to go on can make you half crazy. It's amazing how many people have put pictures of old barn roofs out there. I didn't even find it by searching for Barbasol on the roof. I found it simply by looking at *everything*. I stumbled across it almost by accident, but I did find it. Thankfully the poster had taken the time to list the town in which the barn itself was located. I had been right in the general direction, right in which side of Route 50, but quite a bit off on my general area. I had originally formulated what I thought would be an ideal location based on the math between Sister Bertha's murder combined with both Trudy and Susan's disappearances and then expanded a hundred miles around it.

Using my cell phone I ran a Google Maps trip to the location. The results came back a six hour drive. I thought I could do it in a little over five, if I was lucky. Grabbing my laptop I headed for the door.

There was a gas station just down the road. I tanked up and grabbed a couple Monster Energy Drinks for the road.

"Those will kill you," Sister Bertha said as I slipped in behind the wheel.

"I've got cancer," I reminded her. "I'm already dead, sooner rather than later."

## 8

It was just a little past two in the morning when my headlights picked up the first hand painted sign planted on the highway. The same faded white with red letters proclaimed THE RESURRECTION CHURCH TENT REVIVAL, and down the road the second: TWO DAYS ONLY! A smaller freshly painted sign beside it read, BARBASOL FIELD 7PM! I turned on to the cut-off that followed. Moments later I was looking at a broken down long deserted barn with its roof advertising Barbasol Shaving Cream in faded paint. Across the field, stood the shabby patched tent. It looked more dilapidated than I remembered. In fact it looked almost sad and desperate. The folding chairs were still under it. The makeshift stage with the rusted sheet music stand that served as a pulpit in the middle were in place. Behind it all sat the white and rust box truck with the banner proclaiming RESURRECTION SPOKEN HERE, in faded red paint once again hung on its side.

There was a semi-warm cup of coffee from the last all night truck stop I'd passed still sitting in the cup holder. I grabbed it and my cigarettes and stepped outside into the morning air. As I lit a cigarette I stared at the old truck. The Prophet was inside, I could feel his presence like a fist tightening around my heart and lungs.

Standing there in the early morning hours the reality of it all washed over me like a cold ocean wave. I wasn't crazy. It was true. It was *all* true. Concealed just inside that truck was something evil, something vile, and something only I could destroy. And I had no idea what I was going to do.

My father had owned a little .22 caliber pistol that became mine when I turned of age. It was packed in my suitcase in the car. It had seemed a good idea at the time. Now, however, I found myself not so sure I wanted to trust the small caliber bullets to end the reign of a demon from Hell itself. I wasn't even sure it would take out his human watchman, unless I got a pure headshot. I considered stuffing a rag in the gas tank and lighting it on fire, but other than the movies, I had no idea if it would work. For all I knew I'd blow myself up along with it…or it wouldn't work at all. I was in way over my head and I knew it.

It had been a long night and I was exhausted. My mind buzzed with so many thoughts, so many thoughts I couldn't hear myself think. The Prophet wouldn't take his next victim until after the night's performance. I decided to find a room nearby and get a few hours sleep. Maybe then I could make sense of it all.

After a bit of driving I found a ramshackle motel next to a twenty-four hour truck stop. The room wasn't much, but it was cheap, had a clean bed and didn't ask for ID when paying with cash. Realizing I hadn't brought a book with me, and I was too wired to just close my eyes, I walked over to the truck stop for a magazine.

Feeling a bit hungry, I picked up a Styrofoam container of chicken fingers and mashed potatoes. Say what you want about truck stop food, you'd be hard pressed to find food like that when most of the surrounding area would be eating breakfast at that hour. With my food container in one hand, I checked the magazine rack and was extremely happy to see they actually carried *Ellery Queen's Mystery Magazine*. Even better, the current issue had a new story by Paul D. Marks.

With both food and magazine in hand, I happily walked across the parking lot to my room. When I entered, Sister Bertha, Susan and Trudy were waiting for me, their flesh shrunken and showing signs of decomposition. A thought crossed my mind and I laughed under my breath.

"What's so funny?" Sister Bertha wanted to know.

Setting the food down I looked at them, feeling embarrassed. "Sorry," I said, "but all those times as a teenager I dreamt of being in a motel room with three women…"

A smile crossed Sister Bertha's face. At least it seemed to. Given the fact that her lips had shrunk back away from her teeth, I couldn't be sure. "A little too late," she said.

Dropping the food on the nightstand, I stretched out on the bed with my magazine.

"So what's your plan?" she asked.

"I don't have one," I admitted. "This is the first time I've ever decided to kill a demon. I'm going by gut feeling."

"And?"

In lieu of an answer, I only yawned. "Excuse me," I said and the world went black.

When I woke, it was nearly four in the afternoon. My food was cold, but thankfully I don't mind cold chicken fingers. I had to throw the mashed potatoes away, though. I showered, shaved and put my suit and tie on.

"What are you doing?" Sister Bertha appeared as I was packing my belongings into my suitcase.

"Going to the revival," I told her. "Got to look the part."

I arrived back at the Revival fifteen minutes early. Folding chairs were filling up fast. A lot of people evidently felt they deserved a miracle. After parking the Soul in the field near the Barbasol barn, I took a seat in the back row next to a woman wearing a light purple pantsuit and holding a white purse. Once I sat down I slipped my hand into the right pocket of my suit coat and touched Dad's .22. I didn't actually plan to use it, but I felt better knowing it was there.

Any semblance of a plan had yet to cross my mind. I had a vision of stepping up for a miracle myself, pulling the .22 out and placing it between the Prophet's eyes. But that wasn't going to happen. Whatever I did, I wasn't going to try and destroy the beast in front of a tent full of witnesses.

The Prophet took the stage precisely at seven o'clock. Whatever else the creature was, he was punctual. As I sat there listening to the same generic spiel about his *Lawd*, ad nauseam, my mind just sort of blanked out. Gradually I began to get a feeling that I didn't understand. I knew without a doubt that the woman in purple beside me was sincere. She had come there seeking a miracle. What it was, or how I knew, I had no idea. Maybe she was terminal, a foot in each world, as Sister Bertha had described to me. Or maybe someone she loved was and I was just picking up on her vibe of desperation. Whatever it was, I knew without a doubt that she believed this was her last hope. I snuck a sideways glance at her to see tears rolling silently down her cheeks.

That was when I finally realized what I was going to do. I was going to get in line for a miracle, let the Prophet lay his filthy blood stained hands on me and let him know who I was and that I was there to stop him. I would stay behind until he and his Carney henchman packed up and left. Then I'd follow them.

He was not claiming another innocent life. Not on my watch.

With that decision a chill came over me. What if the Prophet decided to try and invade my mind again? If he did, he'd know I was in the audience. There was no way of knowing if he could enter my mind while he worked his stage, but I wasn't going to take the chance. I spent the rest of the service envisioning myself building a wall of concrete blocks up to the sky. In fact, I was so into my vision, I almost missed the alter call for miracles. The only reason I came back around was that the lady in purple stood up. Startled, I stood and followed her into the line of miracle seekers.

The Prophet took each person in front of him and spoke quietly with them before laying his hands on them. Considering I hadn't hung around the first time I'd seen the Prophet on his promised night of miracles and I was curious. It wasn't until the woman in the purple pantsuit ahead of me stood before him that I was able to hear the conversation. Evidently she had just moved to California from upstate New York three weeks ago, looking for a fresh start after a divorce. Two nights ago she learned that her father had fallen and cracked his head on the concrete. He was in a coma and not expected to come out of it. Her problem was money. After putting everything she had into her relocation, she didn't have enough to fly black. The divorce had left her credit ruined.

Laying his hands on her shoulders, the Prophet told her to stay and see him after the revival was over. He told her he knew an organization that would help her, then he prayed for her strength.

*After it was over?* I knew that meant he'd found his next victim. It made sense. Alone in a new State, no one to miss her right away. Miss Purple Pantsuit was going to die.

When she had tearfully thanked him and moved on, I stepped up. There was no doubt in my mind that the minute he laid his filthy hands on me, he would know exactly who I was.

That was good by me. I stepped up and stood silently before him. "What is it that troubles you, brother?" he asked in his late-night FM Jazz DJ voice.

"You," I said simply.

His eyes showed his confusion only a moment before he placed his hands on me. Then recognition came. *"Canssssssser,"* he hissed through his teeth. The moment he placed his hands on my shoulders I saw the Prophet as he really was. Gone was the thrift store Jesus everyone else saw. The flesh on the creature before me was a mixture of fresh red blood and dried maroon blood in color. Its oversized head stitting on the shoulders resembled a fat toad, there was no neck at all. Bulbous yellow orbed eyeballs with jagged black slashes for pupils glared at me. There was no nose, only two three inch gashes that served as nostrils. Its lipless mouth was open revealing two rows of razor sharp barracuda teeth and a gray forked tongue wiggling like a worm on fire. It was humanoid in form, but its underbelly was scaled dark burgundy like some mutant snake skin. The hands and feet were webbed with long black talons protruding from the ends.

As bad as all that was, its breath was worst of all. The stench of rotten meat mixed with a liberal amount of decomposing fish washed over my face with each breath.

My body became cold, ice cold. I felt the frost closing in around my insides. The last thing I felt before the world went black was the Prophet's hands rummaging through my undefended memory boxes.

## 9

I woke to the strangling feeling of my lungs grasping for air that wasn't there. When I opened my eyes I realized I was in my car and it was sweltering. Sweat poured down my face and into my eyes. The windshield was coated in moisture. The air was hot, wet and thin. Easing my hand to the door, I opened it and allowed the hot, yet fresh California air inside. With fresh oxygen filling my hungry lungs, I once again passed out.

When I woke again, I felt weak, drained of my life's essence. I wasn't sure if it was because the Prophet had harmed me, or if it was because of the heat. Sweat still ran down my forehead. I was seriously dehydrated. According to my cell phone, it was ten o'clock in the morning. Even with the driver's door open, inside the car must have been well over a hundred degrees. Looking outside I realized I was in the field, right where I had parked before going to the revival. No other cars were anywhere to be seen.

"Glad to see you back," Sister Bertha said.

I looked to the passenger seat and there she was. A quick glance in the rearview mirror revealed three women in the back. Trudy, Susan, and the woman in the purple pantsuit. "Say hello to Emily Piedmont," Sister Bertha said.

Shame filled my soul. "I'm sorry," I said, my eyes meeting hers in the rearview mirror.

She smiled sadly and nodded her head, her hand modestly covering her slashed throat.

"What do you remember?" Sister Bertha asked.

"Cold," I told her. "When he put his hands on me it was like being frozen from the inside out." I paused as the vision of the Prophet's real self came back to me. "And he was bastard ugly."

"You saw his true self then?" she asked. "Frog head, bulging snake eyes, sharp teeth and all?"

"And a snake's belly, webbed hands and feet with long black claws," I added.

"You saw his true self. What else do you remember?"

"Nothing," I said. "What did I miss?"

Sister Bertha told me that as I blacked out, the Carney henchman got behind me and caught me when I went limp. He half held me and half dragged me around the curtain. No one in the audience really paid any attention. Everyone was either working their way to their cars, or standing in line for their own miracle. When everyone else had left the field, Emily had gone back up to the Prophet. He placed his hands on her shoulders and spoke softly to her. She too passed out.

The Carney took down the tent and packed it, the folding chairs, and Emily into the truck. He took me to my car and shoved me inside. Then he got into Emily's car while the Prophet got behind the wheel of the truck and they left together.

"That's all I know," Sister Bertha said. "We're bound to you and unable to follow the demon. I assume they dumped the car and killed Emily just as they did the rest of us and left her body in some shallow grave off the highway.

"We sat here all night with you, hoping you'd wake up and chase them down, but you didn't. About four in the morning, Emily joined us here."

Grabbing my cigarettes off the dash, I reached for the door.

"Where are you going? Sister Bertha asked.

"I need to stretch my muscles before we drive," I told her. I'd been sleeping behind the wheel for nearly twelve hours, best I could tell. Both my legs and my spine began to make me aware of that fact.

"Drive where?" she asked.

No sooner had my feet touched the ground and my body stood tall outside the car when the world spun crazily before my eyes and the earth rushed up to meet me. I did manage to twist my torso so that I didn't crack my damn fool head on the ground. As I lay they there in the well trampled grass I realized it wasn't the muscle cramps that dropped me, it was everything else. My heart was racing, my hands shook and my body felt as solid as a bowl of *Jell-O* cubes.

"Still think you should be making a road trip?" she asked.

"No," I admitted.

"Can you drive?"

"I don't know," I admitted. I think so, if I take it slow." I got up, using the car for support, and got back behind the wheel. My body felt somewhere between the wrung out washrag feeling of the flu, and a quivering mass of jelled snot. Whatever the Prophet had done to me, it wasn't good.

After a few trips around the field in front of the Barbasol barn, I felt competent enough to drive back to the previous night's motel. I took great care when walking into the office and paying cash for three more nights.

"You okay, fella?" the clerk asked me.

"I think I might have the flu," I told him. "Best you keep housekeeping away from my room until I feel well enough to leave.

"Yes sir, I'll do that," he said, taking the cash I placed on the counter with two fingers only.

The clerk stood and watched me leave, not moving from his post. As I closed the door behind me, I saw him take a bottle of antiseptic hand cleaner out from beneath the counter and quickly clean his hands. I thought about stepping back in and telling him a demon from Hell had touched me, and if it was contagious, I doubted hand cleaner would do him any damn good, but I continued on to my room.

That was Saturday. The Prophet was on his leisurely way east heading toward his next meal in a week and I was lying in a motel bed with the cold sweats, shaking like a junkie needing a fix.

For three nights and two days, I slept a lot. My sleeping hours were haunted by feverish dreams. In some the Prophet stood before me, beckoning me with open arms. "Come to me," he'd hiss. "I will give you peace." In others he would stand silently and show me a postcard of a western landscape with the words *Welcome to Dry Creek* printed on it. When I would wake, Sister Bertha was always there. I would tell her my dreams. She told me that she'd asked the others in the Prophet's abyss what it could mean. When Monday finally came around I was starting to feel better. I woke sometime in the early afternoon, ravishingly hungry: Although I had drank some water every time I woke, I hadn't actually eaten since Friday.

I walked over to the truck stop and got two Deluxe Cheeseburger sandwiches, and an order of onion rings and a large Coke. The food nearly had me drooling as I walked back to the room. When I entered, Sister Bertha was waiting for me. "Feeling better?" she asked.

"Starving" I told her setting my food down on the desk and pulling up the chair.

"Want to hear a story, while you eat?"

"Sure."

It seemed that during my time of unconsciousness, Sister Bertha had gone back to the lost souls in the Prophet's abyss, looking for answers. The man I thought of as The Carney was actually named Cecil. He had been the Prophet's henchman and right hand man for about five years. He'd been a hardcore drunk for thirty years prior. In fact, it was his being diagnosed with liver failure that prompted him to follow his wife to a Resurrection Church Tent Revival in the first place. Facing death, he thought he should seek a miracle, evidently. The Prophet had laid his hands on Cecil's shoulders and told him the cost. Cecil convinced his wife they needed to stay behind after the service to talk with the Prophet. He was, he told her, a changed man. He was. He wasn't actually healed, per se, no one was, but his liver problems were frozen in time. It was still there, but it wouldn't progress any further. Given the right circumstances, Cecil could live to a ripe old age, his liver would always bother him, but it wouldn't be what killed him.

For the miracle of freezing his liver damage, Cecil had offered his life in servitude to the demon. Not to mention that of his wife, whose life's essence was bled out that very evening. Cecil's wife had seen him slit the throat of the Prophet's previous servant moments before the Prophet had placed his hands on her head. It was the last thing her earthly eyes ever saw. Cecil's problem was he never quit drinking. I remembered smelling the whiskey on his breath the first day I met him.

That seemed to be the Prophet's general plan: get someone on death's door, heal them and use them until they were no longer needed. The overall consensus from Sister Bertha was that I was being groomed to become Cecil's replacement.

"So," I said finishing off my second Cheeseburger, "You are telling me the Prophet expects me to murder Cecil and become his replacement?"

"It seems that way, given the visions he's sending you."

"Maybe he's just trying to set me up for a killing myself."

Sister Bertha looked thoughtful, at least as thoughtful as a decomposing corpse could. "No," she finally said. "If he'd wanted you dead, he had the chance. He wants you to serve him. He's trying to sell you on the idea."

"And all I have to do is murder his current servant, drive him around, set up the tent show, and lead a lamb to slaughter." With my meal finished, I grabbed my cigarettes and stood up to go outside and smoke.

"When facing the certainty of their own death, there are people who wouldn't give it a second thought if it meant prolonging their own existence," she said.

Opening the door, I considered this. "Survival of the Worthless."

As I smoked outside, I watched the faces of the other people coming and going in the parking lot. I knew nothing about anyone there, yet I understood that each face I saw could at some future time be strung up and bled out like livestock to feed some creature from Hell, and no one would be the wiser. No one except me.

When I was finished smoking I stepped back into the room and grabbed my car keys.

"Where are you going?" Sister Bertha asked.

"To find a sporting goods store," I said. "It's time to finish this."

## 10

It took some time to find a sporting goods store, but I wasn't in a hurry. Sister Bertha had not accompanied me, probably because she knew I needed to work things out. I eventually found a store and bought what I'd wanted, and a few more items that grabbed my eye. I drove around for a couple hours, trying to get my head around what I was going to do before stopping by a KFC for dinner and taking it back to the motel.

Once back inside my room I was happy to see Sister Bertha was nowhere around. I opened my chicken dinner and sat down before my laptop. After better than a half hour I came to the conclusion that there simply wasn't, or was there ever, a town called Dry Gulch in California. There was a campground in Sierra National Forest by that name but it was way too far south, and it didn't seem likely the Prophet would be leading me to a public place. I was about to give up, believing it was only a fevered dream after all when I stumbled upon a place called the Dry Gulch Ranch on a website of abandoned California oddities. The Dry Gulch Ranch Studio had been built as an independent movie location back in the late thirties when everyone with a camera and a horse was pumping out sixty minute westerns. It was the time when John Wayne was just learning his cowboy swagger. Although The Duke never filmed a picture there, Ken Maynard shot a few.

A small street with interchangeable signs on the buildings that allowed each production to create a new frontier town as needed, a couple small cabins to the side for homes and a small, but decent soundstage on property for indoor location shots, all surrounded by acres of wilderness and dusty trails. All of this was located far enough off the beaten path so as not to have civilization intrude by way of trains, planes or loud trucks rolling by. The few pictures shot there were reportedly completed in three days at most. It was a perfect location for an independent studio with little money and a willingness to drive the distance to save money.

The problem was timing. Dry Gulch Studios only had about three years before the golden age of cheapie westerns had passed. The studio went bankrupt and the property sat abandoned for nearly thirty years until a group of investors bought it in the seventies, spruced it up and turned it into the Dry Gulch Ranch Studio Park. The idea being to recreate the Old West experience complete with gunfights in the street, bank holdups, jailbreaks, stagecoach and horseback riding. Once again the timing was late. Americans wanted roller costars, *Disney* Characters and flying teacups in the seventies, not college students playing cowboy. The business folded in its first year, the buildings left to fall apart and property reclaimed for back taxes. Given its secluded location, even the graffiti artists and general vandals didn't make the journey. And it fit into what I'd come to think of as the Prophet's eastward path along route 50

It was perfect.

I realized then that although I hadn't given a lot of thought to it, I had believed that the Prophet drove aimlessly between points, maybe sleeping in rest areas. This new revelation made me realize he had a plan and a route. He must have safe places along that route to hide away in between revivals. He'd been doing this for a long-long time, it was only natural he had resting places. According to Google Maps, it was about a six hour drive away.

My mind was abuzz with electricity. I knew I'd never sleep, but I knew I needed to rest before I began. I'd been dreadful sick for nearly three days after the Prophet touched me and I didn't need to run off half cocked.

I poured two fingers of bourbon and took a long hot shower, followed by another two fingers from the bottle, before climbing into bed with the copy of *Ellery Queen's Mystery Magazine* I'd bought. I got through three and a half stories before I fell asleep. I knew then what I was heading into. I was going to follow the visions in my dreams based on a consensus of dead people, and try to kill an actual demon from Hell.

Sleep came fitfully, but it did come to me. I dreamt not of the Prophet, exactly. Instead I found myself in the past, back at some generic tent revival with my parents. I was sitting there between them, reading my comic book. On Sundays they went to church and I had Sunday School. Dad insisted that was enough "churchin" for any young boy. Mom didn't like the idea of me reading comics at the revival but Dad insisted. He always passed me a new comic with a wink of his eye. "There you go, Corney," he'd say. "You'll get your churchin' this Sunday. Tonight just read your comic and try not to get too antsy in the pantsy."

Somewhere during the service, I looked up to see the preacher looked a lot like the painting of Jesus in our church. I was staring at him when my father leaned down and removed the comic book from my hand. "Be careful of this one, Corney," he whispered. "This one *bites*."

I woke up after that, covered in sweat.

This dream was repeated three or four times, I can't really remember. Each time I got up, got a drink of water from the bathroom sink and went back to bed, trying to think of happier things. Each time I wound up back at that revival.

Finally I got out of bed a little after seven o'clock. Even though I'd showered before going to bed, I opted for another. Waking up all those times in a cold sweat left me feeling grubby. I turned the water on full hot; enough to make my skin turn pink, and tried to scrub the memory of the dream away. Standing there under the scalding water I realized my stomach was nervous. It was almost the nervousness you got just before getting on a dangerous looking rollercoaster, but not quite. There's a fine line between excitement and actual fear. I was scared. On one hand I realized I was scared because I hadn't seen Sister Bertha in awhile. Maybe it was all in my mind. Maybe I was going crazy and didn't even know it. On the other hand I was scared because I knew I wasn't crazy at all. I knew in my heart of hearts I was going to hunt a demon with nothing more than a few items picked up at the sporting goods store. Those, and my father's little .22 caliber pistol.

At least the shower had the desired effect. I stepped out feeling much better than I had getting in. It didn't take long to pack my few belongings into the car and I stepped over to the truck stop. I had considered having a sit-down breakfast of bacon, eggs, potatoes and some wheat toast, but I knew I'd get *antsy in the pantsy*. Instead I settled on something they called the Breakfast Chopwich. A boneless pork chop between two fried eggs with fried onions and cheese on top, all packed into a homemade biscuit as big as my fist and a large coffee with an extra caffeine shot for good measure.

At the counter they also offered a fine selection of older CDs designed to keep truckers motivated at a cheap price. I found *Appetite for Destruction* by Guns N' Roses, *Look What the Cat Dragged In*, by Poison, and a copy of something I remembered my father playing, *Roadwork* by Edgar Winter's White Trash. With a belly full of pork chop, eggs, biscuit and high octane coffee, along with ears full of very loud rock and roll, I headed down Route 50.

It was a little past three in the afternoon (including a break for lunch) when I reached the exit off Route 50. After that I drove about ten miles on a secondary road before the GPS informed me I had arrived. I sat on the road edge looking at a long ago paved road that nature was trying to recapture. It was no surprise that a theme park didn't make it, being as far as it was from anything. There was a rusted chain across the broken pavement secured between two trees. I got out and looked at the chain. It wasn't even locked; only hooked to trees on either side. After dropping one side to the ground I got back into my car.

Sister Bertha was there, waiting. "So this is the place?" she asked.

"I hope so. If it is and if he's here, it ends today," I said, as I drove over the chain. "Where have you been? I was beginning to wonder if I'd see you again," I lied. "I was beginning to think I was crazier than a shithouse rat."

She managed a smile. It wasn't pleasant considering the state of her decomposition. "It takes a lot of energy now to actually show up," she said. "But I've been watching you. Can't say I'm too thrilled with that Guns N' Roses CD you played over and over."

I laughed. "So, if he's here, and if I destroy him; what happens to you?"

"I move on," she said. "Me and all those before and after me. We move on."

"To what?"

"No idea. But being here proves there must be something."

"Are you scared?"

She considered this. "No," she said, finally. "Like I said, there must be something. I do hope it's heaven."

"Me too," I told her. "You deserve it."

She chuckled. "What's really on your mind?" she asked. "There's something, I can feel it."

There was. I just didn't know how to express it. "He touched you that first night. Your back was healed, you told me so."

"My pain went away," she corrected. "Never said I was healed."

"But you didn't black out."

"No, that happened the second night."

"You said Cecil was, well, *changed* and yet he didn't pass out. But his wife did."

"I think putting someone out is different from easing their pain or time freezing their ailment," she said. "I think someone is made to pass out in order to immobilize them."

"But you called him a Resurrection Man."

"He is. He can steal you back from the touch of death. Cecil would have been dead in a month, had the Prophet not put his hands on him."

"What about me?" I asked. "I fell out, but before I did, I felt something. It was like a red glow deep down inside me. Was I stolen from death, or just knocked out so he could put me in the car asleep?"

She looked at me. "I don't know," she admitted. If you were *healed*, so to speak, you still have cancer, but it's not going to kill you. Not now, at least."

"When?"

She smiled sadly "How the hell would I know?" A look of pain came over her face. "I really need to go, Doc. Thank you for all you've done."

"If it works, the pleasure was all mine," I said. "If it doesn't, I guess I'll be seeing you soon."

Then Sister Bertha was gone. Not some Hollywood fadeout or dissolve, simply gone. I got out, hooked the chain back up and drove forward.

According to what I'd read, both the original studio and the failed theme park were located three quarters of a mile in from the highway. Watching the odometer I drove for a half mile and shut the car off. Getting out I opened the trunk, pulled on a pair of rubber gloves and retrieved my items from the sporting goods store. I tucked both the eighteen inch machete and the steel camping hatchet behind my back under my belt. The twenty-seven inch aluminum little league baseball bat I held at my right side. Wood tends to soak up a trace of blood, no matter how hard you wash it. Almost as an afterthought, I stuck my father's little .22 caliber pistol into my right front pocket. Finished, I grabbed a bottle of water, opened it and drank half, resealed it and tossed it back inside the trunk. Prepared as well as I could be, I began to walk the last quarter mile.

Keeping my mind as clear of thought as I could, I walked on in silence. Eventually the old road opened up into a large overgrown parking lot. The asphalt was uneven and split, leaving places where weeds grew up between the cracks. The remains of two old Chevy passenger vans sat on dry rotted tires near a large building that must have once been the soundstage and now was not much more than a large box shaped building falling in on itself. The vans might have once been white, but had turned the color of old bloodstain rust with the passage of time. Most of the glass had long since shattered.

Past the old soundstage the pavement turned into a dirt and gravel road. Two houses stood far enough off the road to look like country settings. Most likely the studio homesteads I'd read about. The road took a turn and beyond I saw the western main street. It looked like every western ghost town I'd ever seen in the movies except for the lack of tumbleweeds and the addition of The Resurrection Church Tent Revival box truck parked in the middle of town.

Cecil was sitting under a small canopy tent with his back to the sun, and me. There was a near empty whiskey bottle on the table to his right, the truck to his left. The sounds of old country music wafted back on the air. I think it was Willie Nelson. Given that I was walking on the only access road, I knew this was a regular layover for the Prophet. Why else would Cecil have been so comfortable as to be sitting with his back to the only entrance point to their location?

The closer I got I began to hear Cecil singing along with Willie in a slurred voice. By the sounds of it, Cecil was shitfaced. He didn't have a clue I was walking up behind him. The closer I got, the more I could feel the rage within begin to consume me. What kind of subhuman could destroy his own health and then offer the life of his wife for more time in his own miserable existence; and continue to secure unsuspecting innocents every week just to keep his grub worm heart beating? In a twisted way I despised him more than the Prophet himself. Cecil at one time was allegedly a human that knew right from wrong.

The urge to call out to him, to have him witness his own demise was bubbling up inside me stronger with each step I took. It was only when I saw the handgun sitting beside the whiskey bottle on the table that the emotion was squelched.

Unfortunately I was so focused at the back of Cecil's head, I did not see the empty bottle on the ground in front of me. One glass bottle on the entire dirt main street and I managed to kick it with the toe of my shoe.

The sound of the glass bottle skittering across the gravel behind him caused Cecil to grab for the gun at his right side while he tried to stand and spin around to his left. I swung the aluminum little league bat with all the force I could muster. The bat connected under his left eye, spinning him backward to the ground. Cecil got one wild shot as he fell, sending a bullet into the side of the truck. I looked down to see the force of my hit had shattered the bone under his left eye socket and popped the eyeball out. It hung, looking downward, still connected inside his skull by the central artery and vein of the retina. He stared up at me with his good right eye, as he raised the gun towards in my direction. I crossed the bat over my left shoulder and swung it down against his left temple just in front of his ear. I actually felt the bone shatter inward, driving fragments into his brain. Even though he fell to the ground, Cecil still tried to bring the gun up, and actually got off two shots before the body shivered and went still. Thankfully the bullets sailed past me. Blood seeped from Cecil's nose and mouth. Switching the bat to my left hand I used it to secure his gun hand to the ground. That done, I stood over Cecil and watched the light in his one good eye go dim.

The realization that I had just murdered a man didn't come to me until much later. At that moment I gave it no more thought than you would when you crush a roach under shoe and twist your foot listening for the *POP*.

There was a flicker of movement ahead to my right. I stood straight, turning slightly so my back was hidden from that area. The thrift store Jesus that called himself Prophet strolled through the swinging doors of the Dry Gulch Saloon. It looked for all the world like some bizarre scene from some old Spaghetti Western shot by Alejandro Jodorowsky.

"You're here," he said, spreading his arms wide like Christ crucified and walking towards me.

Nodding toward Cecil I said, "You wanted him dead?"

The Prophet sighed. "Yes. Unfortunately Cecil and his constant consumption of alcohol has become rather a disappointment." He continued to walk towards me, arms still outstretched as if he was about to deliver a massive hug. "Come to me, child," he said. "Allow me to welcome you."

As I walked toward him I stayed at the slight angle so he could not see my right hand reach behind my back and grab the handle of the machete.

"I knew you would come," he said.

"How?"

"I healed you last time you came," he said with a slight smile. "Your cancer is dormant and shall remain so as long as you serve me. How could you *not* come to serve me? You are an honest man Doc. You always pay your debts."

"My friends call me Doc," I said closing the last few feet between us "But you can call me Cornelius." With my left arm I swung the bat upwards as a split second later I swung the machete around toward his neck with my right hand.

I had timed it near perfectly, but the demon was faster than I gave him credit for. He yanked the bat away with his right hand, momentarily distracted, but still saw the machete coming with time enough to block my swing with his left.

The blade cut clean through his left wrist. It wasn't like flesh and bone, it was more like slicing through a lunch sack full of blackberry jam.

The hand itself instantly lost human form and returned to the webbed finger clawed hand of its true self. Black liquid spurted forth from the severed wrist.

Twisting my hand I swung the blade back toward his neck when the Prophet morphed into his true self before me. There was no neck to slice. That fat mutant sized blood red toad head sat solidly on the shoulders. With no neck the blade slammed into the side of the creature's head and actually bounced back. I did see it managed to carve off a small piece of flesh, black oily blood flowed from the cut, but that was all. Fortunately when the human hand transformed into that webbed finger monstrosity; the bat fell from its grip to the ground. I eyed it, wondering if I could get to it in time.

The creature opened its wide mouth, its razor teeth oozing with slobber, the snake's tongue dashing in and out, and let out a banshee's scream. Confused, I stepped back, barely avoiding being raked across the face by its one remaining good hand. In its true form the creature's skin was too thick to penetrate with the machete. And then I saw that scaled reptilian underbelly. Grabbing the machete with both hands I drove it upward between the rows of scales. It slid in easily, aided by the oily blackened blood, with no resistance until I actually felt it thud against its back. I twisted it back and forth, trying for maximum damage and pulled it back out.

The remaining webbed hand dropped to the wound, covering it as if to stop the gush of black liquid spewing to the ground. I drew the blade back and aimed at a space between the scales below its hand and rammed it home again.

The creature screamed loud enough to make me think my eardrums would burst. The narrow pupils in its bulbous yellow eyes twisted into mere slits. Again I twisted the blade, hoping to catch something vital inside. The scream was a mixture of pain and confusion. I don't think the demon had ever experienced pain before. When it reached its good hand out in order to swat at me, I stood back, letting go of the machete handle. It kept advancing toward me with both its one good hand and its bloody stump swinging wildly.

I drew my father's .22 out of my pocket and emptied it into its face. Both of those oversized yellow eyeballs exploded in a mass of yellow goo, but the damned creature still did not die. Even blind, the demon swung its arms searching for my flesh. It stumbled forward gracelessly with the goal of ending my life. The handle of the machete wobbled from between its scales obscenely, like some sexual organ searching for a place to insert itself. Realizing this, I dropped the pistol and launched myself at the demon grabbing the machete handle with both hands.

Using the full force of my own body, I shoved forward with the machete, knocking the demon down to the ground. As I straddled the blinded beast with the machete still buried into its midsection, I reached around my back for the camping hatchet. Finally with a fury and force I didn't know I possessed, I began to hack away the area where the head connected with the shoulders. Chunks of flesh flew, blackened blood sprayed across my face, but I did not quit. I couldn't. Unthinking rage alone drove me forward.

Even as I hacked away at the tough oily flesh, I became aware of four sets of legs standing nearby. I looked up to see Sister Bertha, Susan Applewhite, Trudy Jackson, and Emily Piedmont watching. Their various stages of decomposition made it obvious what order these women had fallen victim to the Prophet.

The hatchet hacked again and again as if it had a mind of its own. First the right side, then the left. The blood sprayed everywhere. My hair was soaked, rivulets of the stuff ran down my face, the ground beneath us was saturated in the black oily liquid, still I swung the hatchet. Chunks of the demons flesh came away, falling to the ground. Its struggles became weaker and weaker, but its screams never lessened.

Finally after what felt like days I had chopped away enough meat to reveal what looked like a thorny dark green spinal cord. I drew the hatchet high above my head and slammed it home. Despite the outer skin being tough, the spinal cord sliced through with no resistance. I watched as the giant toad head separated from the shoulders and rolled to the side.

I felt the earth itself vibrate. Beneath me the creature that once was the Prophet began to shimmer and fade. I looked up to the four women who stood witness to what I had done. They stood there smiling as their bodies faded from my view. No longer the decomposing corpses they had become, but as the beautiful human beings they had once been, before the vile Prophet had taken that from them. Pat Samson aka Sister Bertha looked at me. Even though I heard no sound, I could clearly read her lips as she faded away: *Thank you.*

Exhausted, I stood and looked around. The Prophet was gone, the toad creature of his true form was gone, only the machete lay on the dry ground. Sister Bertha and the others were gone. There was no black liquid on the earth or on me. I was alone in an abandoned theme park with a dead Cecil laying where I had beaten him to death.

The aluminum bat was still on the ground where the demon had dropped it. The finish was splattered with Cecil's blood as well as a bit of his skin and hair. Having washed it extensively in bleach after purchasing it, I knew there was no trace of fingerprints, not mine, not the clerk who rang it up, nor any of the countless people who might have picked it up in the store, I decided to leave it where it lay. If the police ever found Cecil's body, they'd be looking for a murder weapon. Why not make that part easy for them? Originally I had thought I'd clean it again and drop it off at some undetermined park a hundred miles or so away. Some kid would find it and take it home, but that didn't seem right, now.

I gathered my Dad's .22, the machete, the hatchet, took a long final look around, and headed back to my car.

## EPILOGUE

When I got back home three days later Harvey was fit to be tied. "I move heaven and earth to get you in, and you *vanish*?" he said to me over the phone.

"I know, I'm sorry Harvey," I told him, apologizing without giving a reason.

"*Don't* leave your phone," he said, and hung up.

I sat at my kitchen table. Technically I was still on vacation.

The phone rang six minutes later. When I answered Harvey said, "You need to be there at seven in the morning tomorrow. As a personal favor to me, they are going to squeeze you in before office hours." He paused for effect before saying, "And this time, don't make me look bad." Then he hung up.

The results of the CAT scan came back negative. Not to be outdone, Harvey scheduled an MRI. That too came back negative. I sat in Harvey's office looking across the desk at him. "I don't understand it," he said. "You have prostate cancer. Fairly advanced, yet now the tests now show nothing."

"Had," I told him. "I had prostate cancer."

Harvey looked astonished. "What did you do?" he asked. "What changed?"

I didn't want to lie to my friend, but I couldn't tell him the whole truth. "I went to a tent revival," I told him. "The preacher laid hands on me."

I returned to work the following Monday as there was no longer any reason to stay away. Besides, I figured that getting back into the day-to-day routine would be good for me. Harvey was still concerned and had me tested the first of the month for three months, but I remained cancer free as far as the results were concerned. When the tests stopped my mind put the Prophet, Cecil and Sister Bertha on a back shelf. It got so that I rarely thought about those days... Until about nine months back when the corpse of a seventy-five year old bald man named Phil Wedgewood was brought in.

Mr. Wedgewood had been suffering from Alzheimer's disease for nearly five years. Rather than put him in a facility, his wife kept him at home in their two-story house, where she had a gate installed at the top of the stairs to prevent his falling down them. It seemed that Mr. Wedgewood had opened the gate during the night and fallen down the stairs, suffering both a head trauma as well as a broken neck.

I was just about to begin my examination when I heard a voice behind me say, "Well don't that beat all?" My heart froze a beat. It's not often someone in my line of work actually hears a voice in a formally empty room. I spun around to face the intruder. What I saw was a carbon copy of Mr. Phil Wedgewood standing in his pajamas behind me. "I'm sorry sir," I said. "No one is allowed in here. If you'd kindly wait outside." (*Did Wedgewood have a twin brother?*)

It's hard to decide who was more taken back; me at the arrival of someone in my autopsy room, or the carbon copy of the subject standing there. His eyes went wide as his mouth dropped open. "You—you can see me?" he asked with astonishment.

"Well you are standing in the room with me," I said. "Are you related to the deceased?"

There was a moment of silence, then the man broke into a smile. "You could say that," he said and pointed to the body on the table behind me. "I *am* the deceased." He turned slightly exposing the side and back of his head. A large piece of his skull had been smashed open. Brains and blood had leaked out. "Name's Phil, but folks call me Red," he said offering a hand.

I glanced at his bald head. "Red?"

"Bad nickname," he said. "In my youth I had a mop of unruly red hair. The name stayed with me, even though the hair didn't." He looked at me. "Am I really dead?"

"If you are the man on my table, I'm sorry to say, yes you are." I said reaching for his hand. When my grasp passed through his hand untouched, I knew and by his expression, so did he.

"So how come you can see me?" he asked. "I've been yelling at people since the cops showed up around four this morning and no one has heard me, until you."

"It happens to me sometimes," was all I could think of to say.

He looked around, as if seeing the room for the first time. "Because of your job?" he asked.

"Yes." It just seemed the simplest answer at the time, and he seemed to accept it.

"So why haven't you passed on?" I asked.

"Can't," he said. "Maybe because the bitch killed me?" He was as confused as I was.

Looking at the notes I said, "Says here you fell down the stairs, Mr. Wedgewood."

"Call me Red," he said. "I never did like that Mister stuff."

"Okay Red," I said hoping that Roger didn't suddenly walk into the room. "Take me back. You are listed as an accidental death, but obviously something is wrong. Something is bothering you."

"What's wrong with me is my loving wife murdered me," he said. "That's what's bothering me."

"So you didn't accidently fall down the stairs in the middle of the night?"

"Hell no," he said. "My wife woke me up in the middle of the night, walked me to the stairway and told me to try and unlock the gate." He stopped and looked at me, realization crossed his face. "I think she was trying to get my fingerprints on the gate lock."

"And then what happened?" I asked.

"Well, she coached me in how to open the gate and when I did, the bitch hit me with the bat, right here," he said pointing to the open wound on his head. "After that I just fell down the stairs. I think I was dead before I hit the bottom. I do remember standing at the landing watching myself tumbling ass over teakettle down them; with her still holding our grandson's little league bat in her hands as she stood looking down from the top."

"Why would she do that?" I asked.

"Because I had Alzheimer's," he said. "And maybe because years back we took out five hundred thousand dollar life insurance policies on each of us. After five years of me getting worse to the point where I didn't even recognize her, she decided enough was enough." He paused, as if gathering his thoughts. "You know if she'd just overdosed me on sleeping pills or something, I think I'd have been okay with it, but a baseball bat to the head?"

"That sounds pretty angry," I said.

"It does," he agreed. "And it pretty much pisses me off, too."

"Okay," I said. "Can you just give me a couple minutes here?" I asked.

"Seems like I got eternity, now," he said sadly. "Go ahead."

I checked the head wound. He was right. There were two traces of wood in the wound. One would have been the hardwood floor of the landing, the other might have well been a baseball bat. I took a quick look at the body overall. There were absolutely no self defense wounds. No broken fingers, no broken wrists; nothing that would have been caused by someone trying to break their fall. Red had been dead, or at least knocked unconscious before he fell *ass over teakettle*. "I believe you," I said and took out my cell phone.

I called Betty. After the formalities, I told her the reason for the call. "I've got a body here," I said, "a Mr. Phil Wedgewood. He came in as an accidental death. Mr. Wedgewood suffered from Alzheimer's disease and seemingly fell down a flight of stairs."

There was the sound of computer keys in the background and then she said, "Okay, I've got the report in front of me now. Why do you say 'seemingly fell down a flight of stairs,' are you telling me he didn't? I've got the pictures in front of me. There is no way a man gets his neck twisted like that and lives."

"I'm not saying he didn't break his neck, or that might be what actually killed him," I said. "I'm telling you I'm not convinced he fell."

"Says here; his wife woke around three in the morning to the sounds of him screaming, followed by several loud crashing sounds. She rushed out of bed to find he had opened the safety gate and fallen down the stairs. We even dusted the gate. His prints were all over the lock.

"What makes you think otherwise?" she asked.

"No defensive wounds," I said. "Even someone not in their right mind will throw up their hands to try and break a fall. Mr. Wedgewood's fingers were not broken, nor his wrists, nor arms. Not even sprained by the looks of them. I'm saying he was either dead or unconscious before his fall."

I heard Betty take a deep breath and slowly let it out on the other end of the line. "This is a hellava leap you expect me to take, Doc."

"Do you have photos of the head wound?" I asked.

"I do," She said. "As well as the pool of blood under his head on the first floor landing."

"Okay, look at that wound. That is blunt force trauma and I don't believe it came from falling down the stairs. Look at the shape of the wound. Wedgewood was struck with something prior to his fall."

"Can you narrow down 'something' for me?" she asked.

It was my turn to pause. How exactly was I supposed to answer the question without saying a dead guy told me? "A pipe, maybe," I said. "or a club. Something like a small baseball bat. You know, the kind little leaguers use."

She was quiet. I could almost see her studying the picture, trying to see if the puzzle pieces fit. "Jesus Doc," she finally said, "the woman is seventy-four years old. Why would she kill her husband now?"

"Wouldn't be the first time a caregiver spouse took matters into their own hands on an Alzheimer's victim," I said. "Maybe you should ask her."

"You know Doc, you can really frig up a perfectly good day sometimes," she said. "I'll get back with you later today." With that she unceremoniously hung up.

"What do we do now?" Red asked.

"We wait," I told him. "I go back to work, while you go away."

I did go back to work. Red did not go away. But he did remain silent. I busied myself in the examining room while I waited, there was always organizing and such to be done there. Roger came in twice; once to tell me he was going to lunch, once to tell me he was back. He didn't see Red.

A little after two Betty called me back. "Listen up Red," I told him, "but don't say anything."

"Why? She can't hear me, can she?"

"No, but I can and it's damned distracting."

I answered the phone and put it on speaker, telling her my hands were full. "You were right, Doc," she said. "Since you're busy, I'll give you the quick version."

The Wedgewoods had a grandson who stayed with them for part of each summer. A little league baseball bat reeking of bleach was found in the garage. Betty had told the woman the results of the medical exam, told her that it would be better for her to admit the truth than to have the bat tested for any traces of blood that might have seeped into the wood. Mrs. Wedgewood broke down and admitted to hitting her husband in the head and watching him fall down the stairs. She also admitted to coaching him in opening the gate lock. Through tears she admitted to recently learning she herself was in critical health and not expected to live much longer. According to her, she did this to prevent her husband from being left alone and committed to an institution for the remainder of his life.

"Do you believe her?" I asked.

"I'm reserving judgment until we get her medical reports," she said. "Maybe it's true she's sick, I don't know, but it's what the lawyer will say. But if you're asking what my gut says: Yes I believe she was telling the truth, at least in her own mind."

When we had hung up, I looked at Red who was already beginning to fade. "What's happening now?" he asked.

"You're moving on," I said.

He smiled but there was sadness in his eyes. "Guess she did still love me," he said faintly. "Thank you," he mouthed, but this time there was no sound. Then he simply faded from view.

I met with Betty that night and over dinner told her my entire story. I left nothing out. Her police trained factual mind found it hard to accept. I think she might have been thinking of nominating me for the loony bin, but our relationship gave her reason to pause.

As it turned out, Red was only the first. Since that day four more lost souls have appeared both on my examining table and in the room with me. It seems that even though the Prophet hid my cancer from my body, it *is* still there. I still, as Sister Bertha told me, have a foot in each world. I have listened to these people and by passing the information off to Betty she has solved four previously unsolved murders. When faced with the fact that I knew things I had no right to know, Betty came to believe, even if she didn't understand.

As for me, I'm pretty much still boring. I still spend too much time in the company of my noir movies and books. I quit smoking again as it seemed the right thing to do. I also don't have too many chats with Jesse James Outlaw Bourbon because being free of cancer only to develop liver problems was a chance I didn't want to take. I still seem have a foot in each world. The occasional visit from the recently deceased on my table tell me that much. It took some getting used to, but I have come to accept that although I can't actually raise the dead, I can talk to them, sometimes.

I have become a Resurrection Man myself, of sorts.

# AFTERWORD

Resurrection Man began life as an idea for a short story around 4500 words. I have never written a story in first person, and this idea came to me blended from my love of horror and my childhood reading of detective paperback novels. Soon it became evident that the tale demanded more space. Res Man grew beyond short story, beyond long short story until it filled some 32,000 words: Too long for a short, too short for a novel. I couldn't see stretching it beyond where it came to end, and couldn't bring myself to trim it down more, so I decided to release it as this novella.

As I'm known to mention stories are strange things. They are really nothing more than a string of words put together, hopefully with a beginning, middle, and an end that brings it to a satisfactory conclusion. Although they tend to be therapeutic for the author, they are totally useless in the grand scheme of things unless someone besides the author is willing to invest some of their time to actually read the story. This is where you come in. Just by reading this story you have given Resurrection Man its purpose in life, and I thank you for that.

I hope I have entertained you, as one never gets back the time they invested in any story.

Thank you again for sharing your time with me. Remember authors live and die by reviews. If you are so inclined, drop a line on Amazon.com. Until next time, feel free to drop me an email and tell me what you did or didn't like about Resurrection Man at FranklinEWales@aol.com.

Franklin E. Wales, Palm Beach County, FL 11/2019

"Franklin E. Wales is so good at layering words on a page he can write the feathers off a plucked chicken. No lie."
                    Romance Novelist, Jackie Weger.

**Also Available:**

## BOOGER

Not believing in his child's night scares cost David Thurston his child's life. Believing in them cost him nearly a decade of his own. It took the doctors at the Sunnyville Mental Institution seven years to convince David the only Boogeyman was in his mind. It took only a few weeks back in the outside world to convince him they might be wrong.

## GAMEMASTER

A millionaire sociopath sits on death row for his calculated slaughter of several children. Bernard Hopkins is unconcerned with his approaching execution. His only concern is that the world does not know it was his superior intellect that designed the future that awaits them. Are we masters of our own destinies, or simply puppets being manipulated by the GAMEMASTER?

## FRIEND

Four years ago a presence came to Coral Beach, Florida, and has been quietly feeding on the hearts and souls of the population ever since. Now the time has come to harvest what has been sown. As the death toll rises in an orgy of spilled blood, all that stands between this evil and the town is a broken-down pastor and his handful of life's castoffs. To win they must first understand what they are facing. To lose means to bring Hell to Earth.

## DEADHEADS: EVOLUTION
### Featuring original illustrations by Joseph "Jody" Adams

It's been two and a half years since the Deadhead Virus was let loose, raising the dead to walk the earth in search of human flesh. Now, as the remnants of humanity try to rebuild in the land of the living dead, legends are whispered of a warrior, part human, part Deadhead, who walks the line between both worlds. The Deadhead race is evolving…

## PURGATORY JUNCTION
### In the tradition of the Spaghetti Western:

Benjamin Midkiff.............The Bounty Hunter
George "Dealer" Grant............The Gunslinger
Forest Bishop.........................The Land Baron
Jennie Stevens....................The Saloon Owner
Cain Hartford..............................The Gambler
Pastor Tobias................................The Preacher

All six will suffer in Purgatory…Only one shall survive.

## EATON FALLS

The township of Eaton Falls, New Hampshire has a dark history. Legends vary on its beginnings; some say it was an unknown virus, rabies, or starvation that brought the madness. Stories even more sinister are told in whispers. They all, however, end with the Christmas Eve massacre that left nearly half the townspeople dead.

Now a hundred years later, the sins of the forefathers will be laid upon their offspring. Vengeance will be demanded, blood will be spilled and lives changed forever.

## SAILOR'S COVE:
### A Tale From Prosperity Glades

Like many small towns, Prosperity Glades keeps its dark secrets hidden away from the prying eyes of outsiders. The Sailor's Cove Private Resort is one such secret. Built in the nineteen fifties at great expense, its doors never opened to the public. Over the years, memories of its existence faded away, just as the iron fence surrounding the property disappeared under decades of overgrown vines and greenery.

## THE DRAMOS SAGA

They slaughtered his village in a frenzy of bloodlust and cruelty.
He followed them to America, vowing vengeance.
His name brings fear to the Undead, for they know of his wrath.
His name is Dramos and this is his Saga.

Made in the USA
Columbia, SC
14 June 2022